THE WINE ROOM
MURDER

THE WINE ROOM MURDER

Stanley Vestal

COACHWHIP PUBLICATIONS

Greenville, Ohio

To
FRANK A. REID
For Auld Lang Syne

The Wine Room Murder, by Stanley Vestal
© 2013 Coachwhip Publications
Walter Stanley (Vestal) Campbell, 1887-1957
No claims made on public domain material.
Published 1935.
Cover: Glass of Wine © Nikola Bilic

ISBN 1-61646-225-6
ISBN-13 978-1-61646-225-3

CoachwhipBooks.com

tu lene tormentum ingenio admoves
plerumque duro; tu sapientium
curas et arcanum iocoso
consilium retegis Lyaeo;

Horace, *Odes*, III, 21

CHARACTERS

MR. MERTON	*Narrator of Story and Friend of Congreve*
GEORGE CONGREVE	*Connoisseur and Buyer of Wines*
EUGÉNE, VICOMTE DE MANNY	*Owner of Vineyard of Château Roet*
EVERETT ARNO (*ALIAS* GOOSY RAUH, AMERICAN BOOTLEGGER)	*Would-be Purchaser of Vineyard*
BERTIE MONKHOUSE	*English Nephew of the Vicomte*
MADAME FÜRST	*Friend of Monkhouse*
FUGGER BEY	*German, Interested in Chemistry of Viticulture, Employed by Arno*
RICHARD LEWIN	*American, Buying Wines for Private Use*
BUTCH MARTY	*Lewin's Bodyguard*
JULES, A GASCON	*Keeper of the Wines of the Château*
MRS. LEWIN	*Mrs. Lewin's Companion*
MISS SIMPSON ROBERT	*Butler at Château*
HENRI	*Vicomte's Chauffeur*

CONTENTS

Part Three: The Solution

PART ONE
THE FACTS

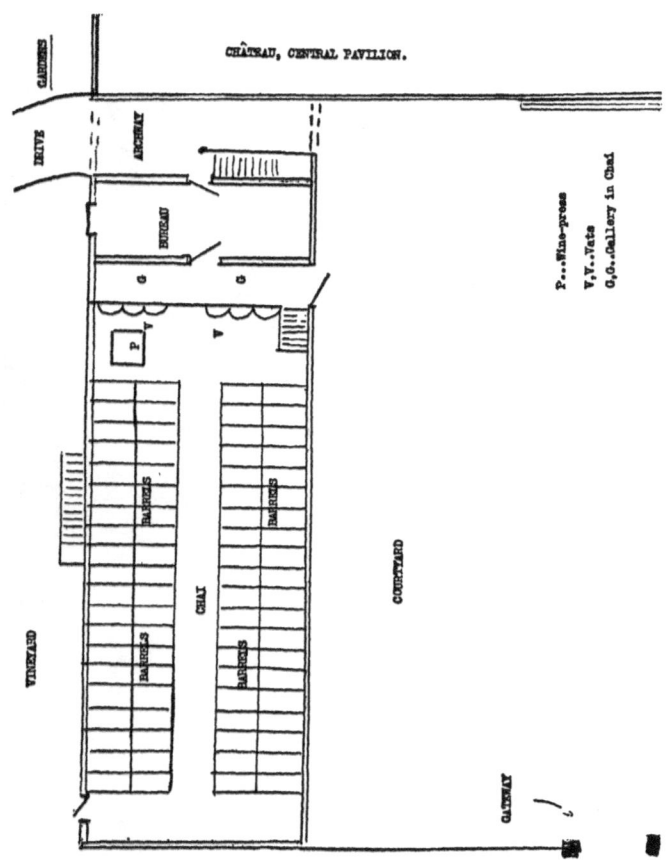

CHÂTEAU, CENTRAL PAVILION.

P...Wine-press
V,V..Vats
G,G..Gallery in Chai

CHAPTER I
CHÂTEAU ROET

THE MYSTERIOUS MURDERS at Château Roet—bizarre and baffling
though they were—did not attract, in the United States, the attention they deserved. At the time they became news, France was in
turmoil. Rumors of war, the crash of cabinets, Royalist riots, grave
financial scandals, the fall of the dollar—all these major events
inevitably filled the front pages of American newspapers and
crowded mere murder stories into oblivion. There was, besides, a
concerted effort on the part of certain French winegrowers to hush
up the affair in the interest of their American trade, then just opening again after the repeal of the Eighteenth Amendment. Moreover, the mystery was solved before the crimes were made public.
And so it was only the sensation of a day.

Nevertheless, the story of the solution of these strange and
barbarous crimes is well worth telling. And since it is certain that
the indolent gentleman who solved them will never take the trouble
to relate the details, that labor falls to me. I was with him during
the whole of that brief, anxious, and dangerous time spent in un-
raveling the problem and in bringing the criminal to justice. Moreover, we both feel that a straightforward account of the facts, as
they came to light, is no more than an act of justice, as well as a
service to all American wine-lovers.

The ill-advised attempt of the French winegrowers to hush up
these murders could not, of course, perfectly succeed. The result
is that a shadow has been thrown over the fair fame of a noble
vintage—a wine renowned for fully fifteen hundred years—I mean

11

the claret known as Château Roet. Had the crime not been traced to its perpetrator, that vineyard must have fallen into utterly unworthy hands, and the reputation of its wine—a reputation built up by centuries of careful work—would have been destroyed, and multitudes of American wine-lovers defrauded. That disaster, happily, was averted. The world is entitled to know how. . . .

In my opinion, there are no greater blessings on this earth than old friends and old wine. And so, when George Congreve wrote to me from Bordeaux, advising me to drop my scribbling at Cagnes-sur-Mer and join him for a month's tour of the vineyards, I hastened to comply. For Congreve is not merely an old friend and a connoisseur of wines, but a thoroughly civilized person with a flair for the curious and interesting in human nature. I like to think of him as seated at his favorite table outside the café, sipping his *apéritif*, and watching mankind go by with a thoughtful, alert, and not unsympathetic eye. I knew that, wherever George Congreve might be, there was sure to be sound wine, good talk, and a ripe attitude towards life. For, as you will see, my friend Congreve is a man who takes his time.

I did not find him at his hotel in Bordeaux when I arrived there. But he had left a note for me. A car was waiting, and so, after an hour's pleasant drive through the vineyards—then glowing golden brown under the late sunlight of a fine September afternoon—I found myself rolling through the imposing iron gateway of Château Roet. My car circled the sloping, graveled court, stopped before a flight of steps, and I found myself in the shadow of an ancient seventeenth-century façade. I got out and looked about me. The court was empty. But in the long, blank wall of the wing which flanked the court on my right, I noticed a great door standing open on the blackness within. And as the car swung away, a familiar figure appeared in that doorway.

It was my friend Congreve, plump and deliberate. Seeing me, he came out into the fading sun light, and I saw that he had not changed at all since our last meeting in Paris. His coat was as well cut and as comfortable, his linen as fresh, his tie as inconspicuous, his intelligent, good-natured face as smiling and genial as ever.

He came towards me slowly, his eyes alight. I had to laugh, his appearance was so entirely in character. For in his hand he held a stemmed wineglass, clear as crystal.

The glass was empty, and as he advanced, he brandished it gently in my direction. As soon as he was within reach, he pressed the glass into my hand.

"You arrive in good time, Merton," he assured me. "No time to talk now. Come into the *chai*. My friend the Vicomte is about to preside over the ceremony of degustation. To-day we are privileged to taste the vintages of Château Roet from the wood!"

He turned and led the way.

Together we entered the wide door, and I found myself in the cool, cavernous *chai*. Coming so suddenly from the bright sunlight, I could at first see nothing in the darkness. If it had not been for Congreve, I might have met with a serious accident. But he saw me groping blindly forward, caught my arm, and called out, "Mind the steps!" And so I was able to halt just in time.

Of course, I had not expected a stair, knowing very well that in the Bordeaux region wines in the wood are never stored in cellars, but in large rooms aboveground, known as *chais*. In fact, Château Roet was no exception to this rule. But, as it happened, the Château was built upon a gentle hillside. And so, though the floor of the *chai* was level with the road at the gateway, the slope of the courtyard outside made a stair necessary at the upper end of the long room, where the door was. I paused at the top to accustom my eyes to the gloom.

At first I could only make out half a dozen narrow windows high up in the wall opposite, through which a gray light entered, filtering through the dust and cobwebs of centuries. Then I caught the outlines of the wine press, and soon after distinguished several great vats or hogsheads just below me, into which the must had been poured to settle before being drained off into casks for aging. Then I observed a lighted candle bobbing about at the far end of the long, navelike room, and the shadows of a company gathered about it. I began to get my bearings. I followed my impatient friend down the unrailed staircase and stood upon the earthen floor.

There our progress seemed blocked by rows of casks and barrels, all reposing side by side upon low racks, bungs up, for the whole length of the room. But Congreve knew his way about. He led me to the central aisle, and a few seconds more brought us to the company assembled for the rite of tasting.

There the Vicomte, whom Congreve greeted familiarly as Eugéne, master of ceremonies, made me welcome briefly. In the half dark, I could just see that he was a short, stout, self-important, oldish man, with gray bristling hair, who spoke and moved quickly, like one used to making his own decisions. For the rest, I had only time to observe that the group consisted of a fashionably dressed woman and half a dozen men.

There was the usual handshaking all round: to begin with, I met a dapper, black-browed, swarthy American, introduced to me as Mr. Everett Arno; then Monkhouse, a tall, bored-looking Englishman, the Vicomte's nephew, who shifted his stick and gloves to give me two fingers and an "Ah-de-do; a lady in white fox fur, Madame Fürst, who greeted me amiably in French; a tall, blond, bearded, smiling German, who bowed stiffly from the hips, Fugger Bey; a heavy-jowled, portly American business man, named Lewin; and close beside him Marty, a stocky fellow with a hard grip and a suspicious eye, who kept one hand in his coat pocket. I made the rounds and returned to my place beside Congreve. Had I foreseen what was to follow, I should have studied the party more closely. But at the time, I confess I felt but slight interest in that silent circle of chance-met strangers; my mind was intent upon the wine-tasting about to begin. It is not every day that one is permitted to sample the authentic vintages of such a celebrated growth. My imagination was heated by anticipation.

Perhaps it was the dimness of the great *chai* that released my fancy. But at that moment I seemed to feel past centuries breathing round me. Though I could not lay claim to an expert knowledge of the wines of France, I knew quite enough of the history of that famous vineyard to feel the importance, the solemnity even, of that instant. When Julius Caesar led his legions into Gaul, vines were already growing on that hillside. Later, Roman emperors

forbade the importation of its wine into Italy, in order to protect
the Italian winegrowers from the overwhelming competition of its
surpassing quality. For centuries, it was reserved for the table of
the Cæsars. Charlemagne, who abhorred alcoholic excess, relaxed
the strictness of his edict to allow his paladins to fire their hearts
with this noble vintage. Great Popes, such as Clement V, held this
wine in honor. Richard of the Lion Heart and the Black Prince loved
it as they loved chivalry, and for generations the kings of France
laid it down in the royal cellars. Cardinal Richelieu, that connoisseur of all that made life worth living, favored this wine with his
discriminating approval. Experts the world over esteemed it. The
good, the great, the wise—poets, soldiers, statesmen, philosophers,
artists, saints—had known and loved this wine and by it had been
inspired to lofty thoughts and noble deeds. All this I knew. Moreover, I was well aware that the present owner of the vineyard, the
Vicomte de Manny, had labored to maintain the ancient standard
of quality—not without success. And now, for the first time, I was
to taste this noble wine from the wood.

One may be pardoned for growing lyrical at such a moment. It
comes all too seldom.

In close attendance upon the Vicomte a burly Gascon, wearing
a faded blue blouse and a black cap, moved among the casks, armed
with a thin glass contrivance. His air of surly authority, his
weather-tanned, heavy face and gray handle-bar mustaches could
belong to one man only at Château Roet: I knew him at once for
the *maître de chai*, the keeper of the wines of the Château. The old
man's sense of his responsibility and importance showed in every
movement of his body. He moved at his own pace, apparently heed-
less of the fussy, peremptory behavior of his employer, the Vicomte.
Moving among the casks, he halted before one of them, stooped,
removed the bung, and inserted his glass contrivance. Soon after,
he straightened again, and held it up, filled with the lifeblood of
the grape.

Apparently the Vicomte could not have been more excited had
it held his own blood instead of that of his grapes. He was at once
proud, solicitous, dramatic. Having been served first of all, the

Vicomte held his glass towards the light and sighed with satisfaction. He seemed to forget everything else.

The Gascon turned to the nearest guest, the Englishman, and offered to serve him. Monkhouse did not stir to accept the service, but with a quick gesture and a word of. command, he indicated the lady.

The burly Gascon turned towards her to pour into her glass this precious product of the skill and character of ages. His master, the Vicomte, also came forward, holding his candle high for her convenience. Then, suddenly, both men stopped short and stood motionless, staring at her.

All eyes turned to the lady, now plainly visible in the light of the Vicomte's candle.

She stood there, very slim, and elegant in a public sort of way. A woman nearing thirty, as I guessed, incredibly blonde, incredibly painted, unnecessarily smart, insolent, sure of her power over men—all men. Though her dress was not more revealing than the fashion required, there was that about her which made her seem indecently exposed, almost naked. About her shoulders her white fox fur caught the light. An empty glass glinted in her right hand. In the other, she poised a long holder containing a glowing cigarette. A faint blue cloud of smoke was floating from her assured, smiling, scarlet lips. She seemed pleased with the attention of the company; the moment was her own.

The Vicomte uttered an exclamation so abrupt, so violent, that, in the silence, it had all the effect of an explosion. The light of his candle was thrown strongly upon the right side of his florid face, and I could see the veins on his temple swelling with indignation. He stepped forward and lifted his clenched fist. Almost, I thought he was going to strike her.

CHAPTER II
DEGUSTATION

THE VICOMTE'S threatening posture was no more than a gesture of indignation. With difficulty, he controlled his passion, forged it into words. Yet still the violence of it shook him; his hand which held the candle trembled. Once he began to talk, he was voluble in protest. His voice was hard, abrupt, hectoring.

"Madame Fürst," he cried, "Ah, Madame, you cannot intend this insult to the good wine of Château Roet. Consider well what you do. *Mon Dieu!* This cask, it is of the finest since the War. On it all our hopes are based. You come here to taste this—this marvel—and then you have the imbecility, the effrontery, to cloud your senses with the vile fumes of tobacco. Madame, I insist. Put out that fire, if not for your own sake, for that of these gentlemen, my guests. . . ."

Madame, holding the center of the stage, did not flinch under the lash of his reproaches. Now that she was the center of interest, she assumed a new role. She put on an air of pretty confusion and laughed good-humoredly.

"Pardon, M. le Vicomte," she implored; "it was so thoughtless of me. One acquires the habit of indulging oneself on all occasions."

He glared at her, unbending. She, perfectly cool, leaned forward, brushing, as she did so, the tall bearded German on her left, and quenched her cigarette gracefully against the nearest barrel.

"*Voilà!*" she said and smiled.

Then stepping forward, confident of his forgiveness; she extended her glass.

17

Her distressed host mastered himself with an obvious effort, relaxed, and set down his candle. She was, after all, a woman—and by no means unattractive. And the Vicomte was a gallant gentleman and a Frenchman to boot. He contrived to swallow the indignity.

But the old Gascon in the blouse and cap could not so easily forgive. This painted hussy had insulted his wine, his craft, the work of his life. Abruptly, he turned on his heel and passed her by. She was unworthy of his service.

Madame made a wry face and lowered her glass. Confident though she was of her charms, she knew well enough when they were vain, and was much too easy-going to wage useless war.

But the tall Englishman on her right took up the challenge.

"I say, can't you make your fellow behave? Tell him to serve Madame."

The Gascon paid no heed—probably he knew no English. In any case, he was still boiling with temper. He passed on. The Vicomte said nothing.

After a moment, the Englishman broke out again, his voice more irritating than before. "Damn it, man! I mean to say— You can't treat my friend like this."

The Vicomte shrugged and threw out his hands.

"What would you?" he demanded, bristling. "The good *maître* is in the right. Madame has forfeited his consideration. He would never listen. Moreover, Madame's palate is dulled by her so recent smoking. Presently that damage will be repaired, perhaps. By that time, Jules will have regained his good nature. When that happens, Madame shall be served. But at present, no! I will not give the wine of Château Roet to those who are not able to appreciate it."

The Englishman began to fidget and mutter, and presently gave vent to his annoyance.

"What rotten manners! Ghastly, absolutely ghastly! Well, I suppose that the place is yours still—for a few hours. You can do as you damn please here now, I suppose. And *I* shall do as *I* damn please."

With a sudden nervous gesture, the Englishman plunged his hand into the pocket of his tweed coat and brought out a tobacco pouch and briar. Viciously he ripped open the zipper, inserted the bowl, and proceeded to charge his pipe. Then, closing the pouch, he replaced it in his pocket, took up the nearest candle, and held it to the bowl. Everybody stared, expecting another explosion.

Then Madame Fürst, no longer smiling, quickly shifted her glass to her left hand, and reaching out, deftly took the pipe from the tall Englishman.

"Don't be silly, Bertie," she pleaded.

"I mean to say," he protested. "Give me back that pipe."

She shook her head and held the pipe behind her, out of his reach.

The tall Englishman began to behave like a spoiled child and an angry child as well.

"Let me have it," he shouted. "After all, I was acting in your interest—"

He reached for the pipe.

Then Arno, the dark-browed, swarthy man on his right, grabbed the Englishman's elbow and spun him half round. He spoke in a low, husky, unforgettable voice.

"Quit that, you fool; can't you keep your temper for one day more?"

At the sound of that voice, Marty moved suddenly, but no words followed. I could not make out his face. It was in the shadow.

The Englishman shook off Arno's fingers and turned back to Madame.

"Very well," he said, "have it your own way. I'm going. I can't stick it here any longer."

Abruptly he turned, not toward the upper end of the *chai* where Congreve and I had entered, but to a door in the wall opposite, near which we stood. As he fumbled with the key in the heavy lock, Madame called after him.

"Bertie, where are you going? Here's your silly pipe. Take it and calm yourself."

The Vicomte, who was now cool and at ease once more, called after the young man.

"But, Nephew, you have not tasted the good wine."

"Damn your wine," the Englishman snapped in reply, and jerked open the door. For a moment, I saw a dazzling picture of the sunset vineyard outside. Then he was gone, banging the door behind him.

Madame lost her temper. "How tiresome!" she said.

The Vicomte heaved a great sigh and spoke to relieve the tension of his guests.

"Messieurs and Madame, let us forget this little scene. Our tempers—my nephew's and mine are not of the best to-day. Perhaps I myself am not fit to entertain such a distinguished company. The hard times, you comprehend, have not fallen lightly upon Château Roet. Bad seasons, high wages, and in America the Prohibition have forced us to the wall. Had it not been for the providential intervention from America of M. Everett Arno, my creditors would have had me at their mercy. Now that disaster has been happily averted, and I leave the vineyard in his worthy hands. This very afternoon I go to the notary in Bordeaux. I am assured M. Arno will maintain the good name of the vineyard, and so I am content. But not, you comprehend, entirely cheerful. To part from this home of my fathers, it is not so easy, my friends.

"But now let us proceed to taste the wine, as I promised you. This cask which the good *maître* has opened is of the vintage of 1933. It promises to be a great wine. And we have had no vintage worthy of the name since 1929, as no doubt you know. In '31, it is true, we had a fair vintage, but in '30 and '32, conditions were so unfavorable that I refused to bottle our product at the Château. I sold the entire vintage as *vin ordinaire*. A great sacrifice, you may say. True, but the character of Château Roet must be maintained. Owners come and go, but Château Roet remains. Hereafter, M. Arno will guard this priceless heritage."

From one of the men in the shadows, a curious sound came forth. Something between a laugh and a gulp, as though the fellow had tried to swallow his laugh and had not fully succeeded. The sound had come from Marty. That strange sound, so inappropriate, made us all uncomfortable. There was a silence.

While the Vicomte was talking, the *maître de chai* had moved from one guest to another, filling each glass in turn about one-third full. The smiling, bearded German was served first. He immediately offered his glass to Madame Fürst, who rewarded him with a dazzling smile and gave, in exchange, her empty glass. They whispered together amiably. The dark-browed Arno seemed disappointed at the small quantity of wine in his glass, but discreetly said nothing. Instead, to my surprise, he raised his glass towards Madame, drained it, swallowed the wine, and smacked his lips.

The two men in the shadows came forward into the light to be served. Lewin, a portly man past middle life, extended his glass with an eager, boyish smile and a hand that trembled a little with excitement. Marty was now revealed as a swaggering, muscular fellow with a broken nose, and square shoulders too big for his coat. He was by no means satisfied with the meager portion of wine dealt out by the Gascon. And, unlike Arno, he made no secret of his disappointment.

"Hey, Frog," he demanded. "Don't be stingy. Fill 'er up. I'm dry."

His suggestion was wasted on the old Gascon. But the sturdy American seized the Gascon's glass contrivance and held it until his glass was full to the brim and slopping over.

"Attaboy," he commended the startled Frenchman, and tossed off the young wine as though it had been whisky. His portly companion grumbled something at him, but made no haste to touch his own glass. He had his eye on my friend Congreve, watching his every move. When all had been served, those who had not foolishly downed their wine began the rite of tasting it. It appeared that Congreve and the Vicomte were the only real connoisseurs in the group.

Congreve held his glass by the stem between thumb and forefinger. Holding it so to the light, he slowly rotated the glass, tilting it a little so that the wine washed the inner surface all around. His face showed plain approval as the candlelight shone through the ruby liquid. Then he raised his glass, and lowering his head over it, thrust his nose in to catch the subtle bouquet released by that rotation. Having satisfied himself with its aroma, he sipped a mouthful, and raising his head, moved his jaws as though chewing, rolling the wine around his tongue, mouthing it. Then, puckering his lips, he inhaled through the wine. As the flavor reached his palate, a look of intense appreciation came into his eyes.

Having thus tasted the vintage, he leaned forward and spat the mouthful out upon the earthen floor. Our host was behaving in a similar manner, and while old Mr. Lewin and I imitated their proceedings, the two of them broke into a most animated discussion in French, too rapid for my ears to follow. But it was evident that the vintage of 1933 had passed the test.

The Vicomte then explained that the wines of the Château were kept in the wood only three years before bottling and declared that, as there was nothing in the *chai* at the time comparable to the vintage we had just tasted, it would be unwise to cloy our palates further. Instead, he proposed a visit to his *bibliothèque*—the "library," or cellar, where the bottled vintages of earlier years were laid down, like books on shelves.

Accordingly, we all moved after him up the long aisle towards the staircase. The Vicomte and Congreve led the way. The bearded German and Madame followed. The dapper, fierce-faced Arno was next. Behind walked Marty, while the portly old gentleman and I brought up the rear. As we approached the staircase, the Vicomte pointed out an alcove between the vats where a cooper was at work. He explained that the Château manufactured its own casks, and said the tradition was that the owners of the vineyard had done so since the days when ancient Gauls first taught the Romans to use barrels instead of earthenware amphora. My companion, old Mr. Lewin, seemed keenly interested. He delayed me a moment while he stepped into the cooperage, handled the tools lying there, greeted the old cooper, and brought out a wooden mallet, which he carried away with him.

On reaching the top of the staircase, the Vicomte did not lead us into the courtyard through the door by which I had entered, but proceeded along a gallery built across the end of the *chai*, to a door which led into his Bureau. In this office, he showed us cases containing agates and other semi-precious stones. These, he declared, were abundant on this hillside and provided the peculiar gun-flint taste of the wine grown there.

For a few moments, we all stood looking out upon the golden vines, glowing in the autumn sunset. Then we turned to go, and Lewin reluctantly—as it seemed to me—laid down the mallet he had brought from the cooperage. He was smiling reminiscently.

The door of the office led out into a drive, which passed under the second story of the Château and led from the vineyard into the courtyard. As the group passed through this archway towards the court, a surprising thing happened.

The square-shouldered Marty suddenly swung his right arm forward and thrust his thumb into the seat of Arno's pants. Arno uttered a cry and jumped forward.

His action was so ludicrous that I laughed in spite of myself. But a moment later, I was not laughing. Arno swung round menacingly, his right hand in his coat pocket, which he thrust viciously against Marty's ribs. At once I recognized the gesture of a gangster about to shoot.

Marty also recognized it, but apparently was not frightened, rather delighted. There was a grin on his ugly freckled face as he leered into the murderous eyes of the other. More than that, Marty taunted him,

"Go on, use your rod, you rat—you can't beat the rap in this country."

For a moment, they pressed together, motionless, glaring into each other's eyes. Then Arno relaxed, straightened, and turned abruptly away. Marty laughed.

The portly gentleman at my side stepped forward, grumbling in his slow Western drawl. "Butch, what the devil are you doing? Are you drunk again?"

Marty snorted.

"Who? Me? On one glass of sour wine? Not much. But I had to tell that rat where to head in. I was afraid he might be here to kidnap you."

CHAPTER III
M. LE VICOMTE DEPARTS

MR. LEWIN STOOD stock-still at the door of the Bureau and stared at Marty as though he feared his hearing had failed him.

"I don't think I get you," he said.

Butch Marty scowled and spoke with characteristic impatience.

"Hell's bells, Mr. Lewin, the minute I heard that mug's voice, I knew who he was. Repeal has finished his bootleg racket and the snatch racket is the next best bet for guys like him."

"But why do you say he might want to kidnap *me?* I don't understand. What are you talking about?"

Butch Marty scowled impatiently and answered as though he were speaking to a stupid child.

"Baloney. You're the best prospect for the snatch racket in a thousand miles. A guy wouldn't need no gat to carry you off. All he'd have to do would be to hold up a bottle of vin blink and you'd follow him wherever he went to."

Apparently, Marty's familiarity and blunt tone did not offend Lewin in the slightest. His heavy, impassive face relaxed into a tight-lipped smile, his bald head shone, his eyes twinkled, and his comfortable paunch shook gently with silent laughter.

"Well, Butch," he said, with a chuckle, "you may be right, but I'd never have to pay ransom if you kidnapped me. With a bottle of Scotch, I'd soon have you under the table and walk out."

Seeing me mystified by this curious conversation, Lewin, still smiling, explained. "You see, Mr. Merton, I like good wine. My wife won't touch a drop. It's no fun drinking opposite a person who won't join in. But a man has to have somebody handy to drink with. Mrs. Lewin has a silly idea that I need protection when she is not with me. So we made a bargain. I hired Butch here for my body-guard and now she lets me drink without interference."

Lewin laughed again.

"As it turns out, *I* am the bodyguard. I have to put this sot to bed nearly every night. Seems like he can't learn moderation."

Then Lewin, serious again, turned on Marty.

"Butch, I'm still waiting for your explanation about this man, Arno. I understood that he was a well-known California winegrower."

Butch Marty snorted.

"Nuts! If that guy ever seen California, he was looking through the bars of San Quentin. We was in the same outfit in the War. Arno ain't his name. He's Goosey Rauh, the big-shot bootlegger."

Lewin was startled.

"Great guns! What's he doing here?"

Butch Marty slapped his employer on the shoulder and spoke soothingly.

"Don't let that worry you, Mr. Lewin. I've got his number and he knows it. You seen him jump when I goosed him, didn't you? He won't try to pull any fast ones on you now. He don't want the Frog cops on his trail, you bet. The minute he stops behaving hisself, I tip off the gendarmes."

Butch grinned.

Then Lewin spoke earnestly, looking as stern as his naturally easy-going character permitted.

"That's fine, Butch. Now maybe you can stay sober for a while. But remember, I want no unnecessary trouble. You know why I came to France. Remember: whoever interferes with me will cer-tainly regret it. It's up to you."

"Okay, Mr. Lewin," Butch Marty answered.

But Lewin seemed not to hear his bodyguard's reply. He threw up his head, clapped his hat on, and looked anxiously around the courtyard. "Hello! Where's Congreve gone to? We're wasting time here. Come on, Mr. Merton. I don't want to miss anything."

Lewin started off across the court as though he were trying to catch a train. Butch Marty strode along on his right, one step in the rear, with his hand in his coat pocket, on guard, scowling. I lengthened my stride and caught up with Lewin. As we marched along, Lewin flung questions at me over his shoulder.

"Mr. Merton, is Congreve a real connoisseur? Is the wine here as good as he says? What do you think? How long have you known him?"

I smiled at his doubts.

"I think you may set your mind at rest about that," I replied. "George Congreve is recognized as one of the foremost experts on French wines. He has a palate with a memory."

My words seemed to strike the old gentleman forcibly. He looked at me as though I had announced some great discovery instead of a well-known fact. He said nothing more, evidently pondering my observation. So we proceeded in silence across the court until a woman's voice broke in upon his cogitations.

"Richard, wait a moment."

I looked up and saw a soberly dressed lady standing in our path—a lady in her fifties. Once, in the gay nineties, she must have been a handsome figure of a woman, as they said in those days. But years of fussy idleness and overeating had made her heavy and unwieldy, and her face showed lines of habitual worry, or perhaps sorrow. As Lewin approached, she smiled at him with what seemed a show of affection. Yet I had the unpleasant feeling that she was checking up on her husband, as though wondering how much wine he had drunk. With her stood a tall, blonde, vapid-looking young woman, her companion, a professional ingénue.

"Now, Mamma," Lewin cried in a deprecating tone, "you must not delay me. Everything's okay. Our host is going to show me his cellar."

Lewin smacked his lips, his eyes twinkled.

"This is Mr. Merton, Mr. Congreve's friend, who has come all the way from the Riviera to join our party. Introduce him to Miss Simpson and bring him along. I can't stop now. I've just had a perfectly *grand* idea."

Lewin strode off, leaving me stranded with the two women. I confess neither of them interested me. Miss Simpson, the less interesting of the two, extended a clammy hand which I released as soon as courtesy permitted. But I was not to get off so easily. For, on turning to Mrs. Lewin, I found her gone. She was hurrying after Butch Marty.

She caught up with him. He halted and they talked. At that distance, their conversation was inaudible, and to tell the truth, at that time I had no curiosity about these people. Yet even while pretending to listen to Miss Simpson's stupidities about the weather and the gardens of the Château, I was struck by the expression in the faces of the two of them. Their conversation had a confidential air, and Mrs. Lewin laid her hand on Marty's arm with a solicitude, almost tenderness, such as she might have used towards a son. Even more astonishing was Marty's behavior. Though horribly embarrassed by her public show of affection, and uneasy, as such a man must always be in conversation with a lady, the man's face, red as it was, showed nothing but the most kindly and respectful feeling for Mrs. Lewin.

This little pantomime was soon ended. I made haste to bring up Miss Simpson, and the four of us walked on across the court to a doorway where steps led down between thick stone walls to the celebrated *cave* of Château Roet.

Every one had gathered at the door: Madame and her German; the dark-browed Arno; George Congreve; and the Lewin party. Only the tall Englishman was missing, and already the Vicomte, Lewin, and the burly Gascon had disappeared down the dark stair. None of the others, however, showed any intention of descending. I wondered why and asked Congreve about it. Congreve laughed and drew me aside.

"Some silly notion of our friend, Lewin," he explained. "Your doing, apparently. What have you been telling him about me, anyway? That I am a fraud?"

"Nothing of the kind," I answered hotly. "I merely told him what everybody knows. That you are one of the foremost connoisseurs, that your palate has a memory."

Congreve smiled genially.

"I thought so. Now the old gentleman has got it into his head to test out my knowledge. He has arranged with the Vicomte to select bottles of various vintages, conceal the labels, and ask me to identify them. He says he's 'from Missouri' about wines. It is the one subject he seems to take seriously."

I laughed shortly.

"What damn business is it of his?" I demanded. "Who is he to arrange a test for your palate?"

George Congreve surprised me.

"My employer," he said. "You see, Merton, Lewin is mad about wines. Not that I object to that, of course. It is a thoroughly civilized passion, and Lewin is a whole-hearted old chap. But as to wines, he is like a child in a sweet-shop. It is all more or less mysterious to him. For years he has had nothing to drink but corn liquor and bathtub gin. Now he is turning to something more palatable. At present, he has progressed to the point where he thinks a sweet Sauterne the finest wine in the world." Congreve shook his head but smiled sympathetically.

"For all that, the old chap is no fool—a shrewd old boy. In fact, he has made several fortunes. He takes nobody's word for anything, and quite right too. No man can drink with another man's palate. And so, having heard that I knew something about French vintages, he engaged me to act as his mentor and guide on a tour of the vineyards. I can hardly complain if he wishes to put my skill to the test. After all, my stipend is quite substantial."

It seemed droll to find Congreve earning money in that way. But after all, wine-lovers, like other men, have felt the pinch of the depression, and I knew Congreve's wine bill must be enormous. A palate like his is bound to be expensive.

Dusk was already becoming darkness when the Vicomte and Lewin, followed by the *mâitre de chai*, emerged from the doorway of the cellar. All three of them were tenderly carrying sundry cobwebby bottles. Lewin's old face was fairly beaming with satisfaction, as though he were already smacking his lips over the rare vintages the three of them had ferreted out. The Vicomte, too, seemed to have regained something of his naturally gay and gracious spirit. Only the old Gascon maintained a solemnity suitable to his office.

When he had turned over the bottles to his servants, the Vicomte called us together and made an announcement. He invited us all to dinner that evening. Late though it was, he said, he believed his chef could improvise something better than we were likely to find at the village inn, and he was unwilling to have us taste his old wines without the proper food which should accompany them. He was desolated, he declared with what seemed real feeling, that affairs which could not be postponed made his presence in Bordeaux immediately necessary. He would, therefore, be compelled to leave us to the care of his household for the time being, and, though some of his servants would be celebrating the holiday following the vintage, he hoped we should fare none the worse in his absence. He went on to explain that though he must be absent from dinner, he would return in time to preside over a luncheon next day—a meal truly representative of the good wine and provincial dishes of the Bordelais. He regretted that pressing affairs made it impossible for him to plan the promised feast in detail, but felt sure that he could rely on his friend, M. Congreve, to see that no culinary outrage was perpetrated upon the company at table.

Having had his invitations accepted by all of us, the Vicomte made his *adieux*, shaking hands all round, and then bustled across the courtyard to his Bureau under the archway, where his small, old-fashioned, closed car already waited. I noticed that he shook hands with Lewin only with his left hand.

The group broke up and scattered to dress for dinner.

Lewin asked Congreve and me to wait for him. Then he hurried after the Vicomte, his plump figure grotesquely silhouetted against the glaring headlights of the car parked before the Bureau door.

The courtyard was soon empty except for Congreve and myself. For perhaps a quarter of an hour, we waited. Then Lewin appeared again in the glare of the headlights and we strolled to meet him.

We met in the middle of the courtyard, before the main entrance to the Château. Lewin spoke first.

"Great guns," he said, mopping the perspiration from his bald head, "I haven't had such an exciting day since the market blew up!"

Congreve glanced at his watch. "It is seven twenty-nine, gentlemen. I suppose we had better be changing for dinner."

I glanced round. The courtyard was empty. Already there was a light in the rooms over the archway, and we could see Monkhouse, in scanty attire, moving across the windows.

"Let's see our host off first," Lewin urged. "My watch says only seven-thirty. I like the swagger way the French do things."

As he spoke, the chauffeur went into action. The car roared under the dark archway, blinding us with its lights. Then it lurched forward, rolled round the courtyard, shot through the gates, and was gone out of sight behind the end of the great gloomy *chai*.

Lewin broke out again.

"Lucky devil! Lucky devil! Well, there *he* goes."

We all turned to go into the house. As we climbed the steps, I saw Arno come out from under the archway and walk rapidly towards the gates of the Château.

CHAPTER IV
WINE DINNER

THE WINE DINNER that night was delayed, and we did not sit down until long after eight o'clock. However, it was worth waiting for in more senses than one, and decidedly satisfying for an "improvisation." Of course, one expects a good table in the home of such a *gourmet* as I knew the Vicomte to be.

The mere presence of George Congreve at the board would have set at rest any doubts I might have had that the meal would be well planned. George was not a man to enter lightly into intimacy with persons careless of such things as food and drink. He was fond of quoting Oscar Wilde about the "shallowness" of such people.

George was, after all, a product of those golden days before the War—a man trained in the best traditions of the Edwardian Era. His gayety had deep roots, and he preferred Europe to all the world, and of Europe, France, because it was, in his opinion, the paradise of the adult. His philosophy was that life is made of time, not money. "Time is not money," he used to say, "but something infinitely more precious—something that money cannot buy. One dollar is very like another, but a moment may be priceless in its significance." The multiplication of such moments was, in his opinion, the secret of the art of life, and civilization existed chiefly for their minting. Music, sculpture, painting, literature, architecture, social life—all the things which create such moments and make them memorable—seemed to him the most precious possessions of mankind. And George Congreve ranked the kitchen and the wine press with the studio of the painter and the sculptor's *atelier*. All of them alike produced works of art and together made possible the great art of living.

"After all," he would say, "there are only a certain number of meals to be eaten in one lifetime—only a certain number of bottles to be broached." It was Congreve's belief that a discreet sensuality in such matters not only made life worth living, but was the only means of saving mankind from the gross excesses inevitably brought about by a too strict suppression of human nature. Congreve fully accepted the doctrine expressed in the French proverb that: "If you would know a man, you must see him at table."

All civilized persons, I suppose, share to some degree this philosophy, or at any rate act upon it from time to time, but Congreve was committed to it by reason of his special gift, his palate with a memory. Let him taste a wine and it would be indelibly recorded in the archives of his mind. Other men might enjoy noble vintages, wines of race and breed; rich men might fill their cellars with innumerable bottles of the best: but Congreve, beyond any other man I have known, had the skill to remember. His brain contained a cellar that could never be consumed—an expert's dream cellar of rare and precious wines.

Of course, George Congreve could give you a thousand excellent philosophical reasons for practicing these basic arts of life. For himself, no reasons were required. He enjoyed good food, good wine, and would have nothing else if it were humanly possible to obtain them.

I think it must have been a similar instinct and enthusiasm in Lewin which had brought George into his party. No amount of pressure could have induced Congreve to give up even a month of his life to association with a man caring nothing for the refinements of good living. Inexperienced though Lewin was, Congreve saw in him the makings of a true wine-lover and connoisseur. And he was enough of an artist himself to offer his instruction and encouragement.

The moment the Lewins and Miss Simpson entered the *salon*, Lewin began to question Congreve as to the menu devised for the next day's luncheon.

"I have consulted the chef," said Congreve, "and we have agreed that something simple and representative of the cookery of the region would be most agreeable to the company."

"Ah," said Lewin, "and what is the menu?"

"I will tell you," said Congreve. "Of course, our choice is still tentative—subject to the correction of the Vicomte's nephew."

"Best leave me out of it," said Monkhouse. "After all, the taste of the English and the Americans is not the same. And I suppose you believe the majority should rule. I should think the chef is the final authority in such matters."

Congreve's eyebrows lifted in surprise, but he smiled and went on. For the *hors d'œuvres* we have agreed upon Beurre du Sauternais, Les Saucisses Aux Huîtres, and Caviar de la Gironde. Following this, Moules à la Bordelaise seemed preferable. For the fish, the chef favored Matelote d'Anguilles à la Bordelaise, but I feared that the American ladies might not care for eels."

"Quite right," said Lewin. "A little too fishy for Mamma. She can't abide snails either."

"So I feared," said Congreve. "After that Bœuf à la Bordelaise or Côtelettes de Veau à la Guyenne. And of course, nothing could be better with the wine than Cêpes à la Bordelaise.

"Of course, the Bordelais have no native cheese worthy of the name. For those who care to try something not too alien, we offer Le Poustagnacq. And then there will be fruit and black coffee. You approve, Monkhouse?" Congreve asked.

"I suppose so," said the Englishman. "Have you thought of a salad?"

"Salad?" said Congreve.

"Certainly," Monkhouse replied. "I'm frightfully fond of salad. They grow rather good asparagus in France, you know."

"Of course," said Congreve. "If you insist, I have no doubt the chef could prepare something of the kind for *you*."

"Then let him do it," said Monkhouse.

Congreve's manner became distantly polite.

"I'm sure I shall be happy to ask him to," he assented. "Perhaps you can suggest the exact salad you prefer?"

"Aoh, yes," Monkhouse answered. "There's nothing better than Asperges de Metz, in my opinion."

Even then, Congreve's tone was hopeful.

"With Mousseline Sauce?" he queried.

"No, no," Monkhouse answered, impatiently. "I always prefer vinegar sauce with asparagus."

"As you will," said Congreve reluctantly. "I don't know whether there is an asparagus bed in the kitchen garden of the Château. It may be necessary to send in to Bordeaux. I wonder if you hadn't better inform Pierre of your preference immediately? There's still time before dinner, I should think."

"Perhaps I may as well," said Monkhouse, turning away. "I'll just pop into the kitchen now and give the man his orders." He left us.

"And now perhaps," said Congreve, turning to Lewin, "you want to know what we are to enjoy to-night?"

"All in good time, Mr. Congreve," said Lewin. "But the fact is, I can't wait any longer for that demonstration you promised me."

He swung his right hand towards a near-by console table on which reposed four bottles, their moldy labels concealed by napkins neatly wrapped about them.

"We still have a few minutes before dinner. It would please me and entertain the company, I imagine, if you would oblige us now."

Congreve laughed easily. "I rather expected you would combine the test with the dinner. The wine should have the proper frame of food, you know, or some of these precious bottles may be as good as wasted."

"Huh," said Lewin, with a grin. "But you know what the menu is to be. That might make it too easy for you. I persuaded the Vicomte to select the bottles without any menu in view. So if you don't mind, the boy is ready, and here are the glasses."

"Well," said Congreve, "as you like, if the others don't mind."

"Never fear," Lewin broke in. "Every one's interested, and every one is here. Let's go."

"Monkhouse isn't here," Arno objected.

"Oh, Monkhouse won't mind," Lewin insisted. "Let's go."

Beckoning the servant, he indicated one of the bottles. The boy, opening it with skillful hands, presented the cork and the bottle. Lewin meanwhile pressed a glass into Congreve's hand.

Congreve took his time. First he took the cork and turned it over in his hand.

"Ah," he said, "a 'dry' cork. Rather small and not stamped in the modern fashion. Evidently an old bottle."

Lifting the cork to his nose, he closed his eyes, inhaling gently.

Then, opening his eyes, he declared, "A very old wine, but it has not 'gone off.'"

He extended his glass, and the boy poured out a little into the crystal. The fluid had a delicate onionskin color. Thrusting his nose into the glass tulip, Congreve caught the bouquet.

"I judge," he said, "that this is a Médoc—a splendid old Médoc of the first growth."

"Aren't you going to taste it?" Lewin asked.

"Certainly. But one must not neglect the bouquet. Of course, there are those who say that the flavor of wine is altogether a matter of the sense of smell, and that when one holds one's nose, a great wine cannot be distinguished by taste from *vin ordinaire*. That is nonsense, but there's no denying that the bouquet is vastly important. And now for the wine itself."

Slowly he sipped his glass.

"Excellent," he said. "A magnificent Médoc! *Superbe!* The Vicomte has been generous. It might be almost 1864 or perhaps 1869. Those years are rather similar."

"Ah," said Lewin, "'might be' won't do. No hocus-pocus, man. What do you make of it?"

"It is Château Lafite, 1864."

"Ah," said Lewin. "Now you have declared yourself. Let's see the label."

Whisking off the napkin, he rubbed away the mold and held the bottle up for the company to see. "Score one for Congreve," said Lewin. "Now for the second bottle."

The second cork was unstamped, but of normal size. The color of the wine was dark ruby, shot through with yellow lights.

"The bouquet is faintly musky," said Congreve, "and rather suggests the scent of ripened fruit. It must be Richebourg, 1898."

Congreve took a sip of the wine and confirmed his first judgment by the evidence of his palate.

"Yes, that's right," he said. "Show me the label."

Once more the label was dusted off and submitted to the inspection of the company, and once more Lewin had to admit that Congreve's skill exceeded anything he could have expected.

"And now," Lewin said, "the third time is a charm. I'll bet this one will baffle you."

"One can only hope," said Congreve amiably. "Let me have a bit of bread to cleanse my mouth."

The boy produced the bread, and while Congreve mouthed it, uncorked the third of the four bottles on the table.

The cork presented no unusual features, and whatever Congreve may have thought while whiffing it was not confided to the company. His eyes held a far-away, puzzled look, as he compared its aroma with those of the countless items of his memory. Gently he poured out a little of the red-brown liquid into a fresh glass, thrust his nose into it, and considered long and carefully. Still he gave no opinion to the waiting group. Each one was tense and eager, as though his life depended upon Congreve's success. Finally Congreve tilted the glass and submitted the contents to the judgment of his palate.

"A splendid Burgundy," he said reverently. "*C'est magnifique.*"

Lewin's face relaxed. A faint smile appeared upon his lips, but as yet he said nothing.

The far-away look in Congreve's eyes vanished. He was back with his message from the halls of memory.

"It must be—no, it *is* Clos de Vougeot, 1895. I am sure of it."

"Wrong," said Lewin, with a grin. "Wrong that time. It's Château Margaux, 1900. Well, nobody is infallible."

"That I never pretended to be," Congreve said. "But there *must* be some mistake. I am sure this time, unless my memory fails me utterly. It *can* be nothing else. There are not so many such flavors in the world that they can be forgotten easily."

"Well," said Lewin, somewhat gloatingly, "let me show you."

Taking the bottle from the boy, he removed the napkin and scrutinized the faded label. But it was so crusted with mold and dust as to be quite illegible. Impatiently Lewin began to scrub away with the napkin until the lettering showed again.

"There you are," he said, holding up the bottle without looking at it.

Congreve was sipping the wine again, unable to believe his ears. The rest of us crowded round Lewin to inspect the label.

"Ach," said Fugger Bey. "Mr. Lewin, *you* have made the mistake."

"What?" said Lewin, startled, and held the bottle at arm's length so as to see it better.

"I could have sworn," he protested. "I put the bottles there myself. Some one certainly must have meddled with them. My apologies, Mr. Congreve. You were right, after all."

There, plain to be seen on the faded label, was the authentic inscription, CLOS DE VOUGEOT, 1895.

At that moment, Monkhouse appeared at the door of the dining room, followed by the butler, who immediately announced dinner.

That wine dinner was a curious affair. As I look back upon it, its apparently trivial inconsequence seems as unreal and unpleasant as some weird dream of the sea bottom. Even then, it seemed strange to me. But as I recall it now, it was positively sinister.

Around that table, covered with white napery, with its silver and crystal gleaming in the candle light, were gathered those about to have an unforgettable experience. Death sat at that table with his victim, Madame Fürst, and with them sat the means through whom Death worked.

The doomed woman held the center of the stage that night— brilliant, gay, and apparently happy. She had everything her own way. Indeed, from her point of view, the party must have seemed, at the beginning, almost perfect. For almost immediately Mrs. Lewin and her companion, Miss Simpson, withdrew.

As we came out of the airy *salon* into the closer atmosphere of the *salle à manger*, a heavy odor seemed to fill the room—an odor of incense and water lilies.

Before I could determine who was responsible, I heard Lewin protesting.

"Now, Mamma, you know you shouldn't have worn scent to-night."

"And why not, I should like to know?" she demanded, seating herself.

"Why not?" he protested angrily. "This is a wine dinner. Nobody wears scent to a wine dinner. It kills the bouquet. Isn't that true, Mr. Congreve?"

Congreve nodded judicially.

"I'm afraid that is true, Mrs. Lewin," he agreed. "A strong scent undoubtedly spoils the pleasure of the company."

"Then I'm going," said Mrs. Lewin decisively. "I'll not stay where I'm not wanted."

"Now, Mamma," Lewin broke in, "don't lose your temper."

Monkhouse also attempted to smooth matters over.

"Aoh, I say," he protested, "what's the odds? After all— We'll simply open the windows, and every one will be happy. Don't go, Mrs. Lewin, really."

But Mrs. Lewin was on her feet. Her dignity was outraged.

"Come along, Miss Simpson," she commanded, and swept from the room.

"Yes, Ma'am," said Miss Simpson, and giving the company her bright, vacant smile, trailed after.

"I say," said Monkhouse, genuinely annoyed. "This won't do. Leaves a nasty gap in the table, you know. After all, the ladies mustn't be allowed to leave dinner. Can't you persuade them to return, Lewin?"

"No chance," said Lewin. "Besides, it is no fun drinking opposite a teetotaler. I'm afraid we'll have to do without them."

"I mean to say, the ladies mustn't go without their dinner, what? Robert," he called the butler, "see that dinner is served to Madame Lewin and her friend in their rooms, straight off."

The butler bowed and hurried away. We all sat down.

But the proper attitude for such a feast had become impossible. That unhappy interlude had broken the spell and shattered the frame of mind necessary to the appreciation of such a treat. Good wine, as Congreve was fond of saying, requires a certain attitude of mind for its due appreciation. Fatigue, anger, nervousness, all are inimical to the proper enjoyment of this great blessing of civilization. One must be calm, fresh, and unruffled to enjoy fine wines to the full.

The evening was not promising. Madame Fürst alone seemed to retain the gayety proper to the occasion, and, to give her her due, she did her best to carry the company with her. But it was no use. Lewin was decidedly uneasy and fumbled with his glass unhappily. Arno sat silent and sulky—an unwilling guest—scowling beneath his black brows at Marty, opposite, who gulped glass after glass, as fast as the butler served him. It was some time before Lewin's preoccupation permitted him to notice Marty's behavior. When he did, he rebuked the man in a tactless manner which brought the blood into Marty's jowls. I sensed that Marty was already annoyed with Lewin because of his words with his wife, and Lewin's rebuke did nothing to mollify the bodyguard. I felt that Marty had no place in such a party, but under the circumstances, Lewin could hardly be expected to dispense with his protection. Marty, whose truculence increased with every glass, kept eying Arno with a steady malignancy which boded no good. And before the *entrée* had been brought on, he deliberately began to devil Arno, prodding him, as boldly as he dared in Lewin's presence, with innuendoes and sly cracks. For some reason, Arno made no reply and sulkily ignored the sting in Marty's words.

Finally Marty, who found little satisfaction in the small alcoholic content of the light wines appropriate to the beginning of a dinner, proposed to go out and, as he expressed it, "get something fit to drink."

"A bottle of Scotch," he declared morosely, "is worth all the Frog wines in the world. This stuff is all right for young ladies, but a man wants something stronger. Give me some cash, Mr. Lewin," he pleaded. "I'll go down to the village and get me a drink."

"Be quiet, Butch," Lewin rebuked him furiously. "I want you here. I've got no money on me."

"The hell you haven't, Mr. Lewin," Marty replied. "I know better. You always carry a roll that would choke an elephant."

"Will you be quiet?" Lewin demanded, purple with rage. "Sit down and behave yourself. If you don't like the wine, don't drink it."

Marty growled inaudibly and swept the company with a malevolent eye. I expected to see him on his feet and out of the door the next instant. But Monkhouse once more tried to smooth matters over.

"Look here, Lewin," he threw in, "if your man Wants something different to drink, I see no reason why he shouldn't have it, if you'll pardon my saying so. I know where there is a bottle or two of excellent Scotch. There's no reason why he shouldn't have it, is there?" The Englishman's amiability somewhat relieved the tension.

"Oh, I suppose not. Anything to keep him quiet," Lewin agreed. "Anything to keep the peace."

"Splendid," said the Englishman, "I'll pop out and get it."

Jumping up, he left the room. I confess I was astonished at that.

We discussed the *entrée* in silence, for the most part. Madame Fürst had apparently given up her efforts to charm the entire company and was addressing herself to the Bey, who sat on her left. They chatted amiably together, while Lewin fumed and Arno sulked and Marty hatched rebellion.

Congreve alone maintained an outward air of calm and proceeded to enjoy his dinner in what seemed his usual leisurely manner.

But as the minutes dragged on and Monkhouse did not return, Marty became more and more truculent, for all the wine he had drunk began to take hold on him. Perhaps, had Lewin been more tactful, or had Arno not sat directly opposite Marty, what followed might never have happened. But Marty was not the man to sit and take it, and having nothing to do, he began to pick on Arno once more, nagging him in a low, sneering tone across the table. For perhaps five minutes Arno sat there, enduring Marty's goading without a word. Then, as Madame Fürst turned from the Bey and offered Arno a smile and a word, he broke out upon her in sputtering rage. I did not catch what he said, but it was evidently very offensive. Instantly the Bey was on his feet.

"You shall not insult Madame so," he announced. His tone was harsh, his eyes like gray ice. "I will not permit it."

"You and who else?" Arno demanded, also rising.

Instantly Madame Fürst was between them. One glance at Arno showed her that appeal there would be useless. She flung herself dramatically upon the Bey's rigid figure and pleaded with him in rapid French, drawing him away from the man who had insulted her. Reluctantly the German yielded, and bowing stiffly from the waist, ushered her to the door of the *salon*.

When she had passed through, he seized a silver candlestick from the console table beside him and hurled it straight at Arno's head. Arno, though taken by surprise, ducked as he saw it come, end over end, but the small end of the candlestick struck him above the ear, so that he lost his balance and staggered back, clutching the back of his chair.

"*Schweinhund*," the Bey spat at him, passed through the door, and closed it.

Immediately Arno recovered himself and started around the table towards the salon. But before he reached the end of the table, Marty was on his feet, one hand in his coat pocket, his eyes half closed.

"Sit down, you rat," he shouted.

Arno paused, irresolute and furious.

"Sit down," Marty repeated. "I beat your head off once. This time I'll blow it off. Sit down, and keep your hands on the table."

Arno sullenly returned and subsided into his chair. His clenched fists rested on the white cloth. He was trembling with emotion.

"That's better," said Marty. "You always were yellow, Goosey. But I've got you where I want you now."

By this time, Lewin had shaken off his amazement.

"Butch," he yelled, "behave yourself."

Marty looked down at his employer in disgust. "Aw, hell, Mr. Lewin," he exclaimed, "I know that skunk too well. If you like his company, stay here and enjoy it. I'm going."

Swiftly Marty backed towards the *salon* door, his hand in his pocket, his eyes watching Arno. Reaching behind him, he found the handle of the door, swung it open, stepped through, and closed it.

I half expected Arno to rush after him, but he merely reached out and gulped a glass of wine. Then, without a word, he got slowly to his feet, buttoned his dinner jacket, and marched past the astonished butler into the butler's pantry.

Congreve brought the company back to normal with his calm voice.

"Robert," he said coolly, "I think we are ready for the roast."

The frightened butler pulled himself together and went about his business once more. Lewin heaved a great sigh.

"I'm terribly sorry, gentlemen," he began. "I shouldn't have brought Marty here. He's always raising the devil. Why can't people drink like Christians, I ask you?"

"It's a matter of temperament and training," Congreve remarked placidly. "Lewin, try a glass of this Romanée '99. It would do you good. Try it," he insisted, evidently pitying Lewin's state of nerves.

Lewin endeavored to control himself and sipped the wine obediently. But it was evident that its fine qualities were wasted on him. It might have been *vin ordinaire* for all the appreciation he showed. He shifted in his seat. His eyes strayed to the door. For him, the dinner was ruined. For perhaps fifteen minutes, he remained there, doing his best to control himself and win back to the spirit of the occasion. But it was no use, and at last he got out his old-fashioned gold watch, pressed open the case, and held the dial towards us.

"I'm afraid it's no use, gentlemen," he said despondently. "Such a mixed crowd would ruin any party. I should have known better. You see how late it is—five after ten. Marty will be up to some devilment, if I don't look out for him. Until I know what has become of him, I can't go on. I must ask you to excuse me."

He got up heavily, replaced his watch in his waistcoat pocket, and started for the door. Congreve also left his chair and went round to Lewin's side of the table, carrying his napkin in his hand.

"Perhaps I had better go with you," he said, surveying Lewin up and down.

Lewin halted to protest.

"No, no," he said. "That won't be necessary. Honestly, I'd rather go alone."

CHAPTER V
MURDER

THE LAST OF THEM had gone. Congreve sighed and shook his head with a vast relief.

"Thank God," he said fervently, as the door closed behind Lewin. "Now, perhaps, we can attend to the matter at hand."

His fingers closed lovingly around the stem of his glass.

I laughed. "Our wine dinner does not seem to have been a flawless success thus far. A few more such banquets and I should become a dyspeptic with a sour disposition. I don't know whether to laugh or swear."

Congreve nodded.

"It's really pathetic, Merton," he agreed. "Half a dozen people, apparently adult, mostly well-to-do, rather above the average in education, all at leisure, all certainly pleasure-loving, gather round this board to appreciate some of the finest products of the skill and knowledge of ages. But all they can think of is their own damnable petty affairs. No reverence, no appreciation, no decent respect for the opinions of mankind. One can forgive a lack of appreciation for many of the good things of life. It isn't every one who has the opportunity and the training to know a good painting, a good fugue, or even a good book, but food and drink, Merton, are things with which every man must form an early acquaintance. They are the basic essentials of the good life, as well as of good living. Indifference to them is simply the mark of the beast, of the barbarian. And there is no excuse for it, because the lesson is repeated three times a day. Besides, as the excellent Bishop of Autun so aptly said of the pleasures of the table— What *other* pleasure comes to a man three times a day—and lasts for two hours at a time?"

"Let's hope," I said, "that the lot of them will remain away for the full two hours."

Congreve smiled agreement, and together we settled down to enjoy what remained of the dinner. I glanced at my watch. It was ten past ten. Knowing, as I did, that Congreve never left his bed before it was time to totter out to luncheon, I expected a long and pleasant evening.

But my hopes were dashed, for only fifteen minutes later, Lewin stuck his bald head through the door and spoke in a low, excited voice.

"Gentlemen," he said, in a hoarse, confidential tone. "Come outside. There's something funny going on around here. I just saw a man."

Congreve and I looked at each other. No spoken comment could have expressed the depths of our annoyance. But it was evident from the intense expression on Lewin's face that he would not take "no" for an answer. With a sigh Congreve got to his feet, carrying his napkin, which fell at Lewin's feet. Congreve stooped, picked it up, laid it on the table.

Lewin held the door wide. We passed through and he closed it softly behind me. He led the way across the salon, out through the small reception room, and on to the steps at the top of the courtyard.

"*Br-r-r*," Congreve complained, as the cold wind struck his unprotected shirt front.

I turned up the collar of my dinner jacket and stuck my hands into my pockets. The weather had changed. The wind had risen. Light clouds were flying across the moon. The courtyard lay bare and uninviting just below us. As we stood there, thinking only of our discomfort, I heard the chimes of the village clock tower strike the half-hour.

"He's gone now," said Lewin. "But I saw him, all right. When I came out, he was there by the door to the *chai*. But he's gone now."

"You say you saw a man?" said Congreve; his tone was acid.

"He says he saw a man," I explained, trying to make fun in spite of the cold air.

Lewin nodded. Congreve laughed gently.

"So you saw a man," he said. "Well, that's hardly surprising. There are numbers of them in this part of France."

Lewin turned on us indignantly.

"Don't try to be funny, gentlemen," he commanded severely. "There's something wrong going on here. I came out looking for Marty. I naturally supposed he would be somewhere around the kitchen or the wine cellar. I looked into the kitchen, but couldn't find him. Then I went over to the cellar door. The door was locked. There was no one there. I stood in the entry, looking around the court, wondering what had become of him. Then I saw that fellow there by the *chai* door, in the shadow. He was fumbling with the lock. I thought it was Marty and stepped out into the light and called to him. 'Butch,' I said, 'Butch, what are you doing? Come away from there.' The fellow looked around and stood perfectly still for a moment. Then he beat it to the gates. He kept in the shadow of the *chai*, but I could see him. He looked too tall for Butch, but he certainly lost no time getting out of here. I thought we ought to report it."

"Oh, it's probably nothing," I objected. "Somebody came looking for the *maître de chai*, and found the door shut, and decided to let it go. Let's get back where it's warm."

To my surprise, Congreve did not second my motion to adjourn. For, as we all stood there wondering and silent, we heard the door of the Bureau under the archway bang.

"Let's have a look," he said. "If there's any monkey business about the wine, the Vicomte is entitled to know it. After all, you might say he left me in charge. It may be Marty. But if Marty is right about that man, Arno, there may be more in this than you think."

He led the way towards the great door of the *chai*, Lewin close by his side. I hunched my shoulders, followed along, and stood shivering while they attempted to open the door. It was locked.

"Probably bolted on the inside," Congreve was saying.

He stooped to examine the lock.

"Hello," he said, in a low tone of surprise, peering through the keyhole. "There's a light inside. That's odd. Why should anybody be in the *chai* this time of night?"

"Ah, now you see," said Lewin. "I *told* you something was up. Let's try the door of the Bureau."

The three of us turned and hurried up the slope and passed under the dark archway to the door of the Bureau. Lewin reached the door first and turned the knob. The door was not locked. It opened on the darkness.

"Shall we go in?" said Lewin, in a low voice.

"Certainly," said Congreve. "Why not? Get out your lighter, Merton. I suppose neither of you has a flashlight?"

I fished out my cigar lighter and pressed the button. The flame made a meager light. Congreve took the lighter from me and led the way into the Bureau. As we entered, we heard a car start in the road before the Château.

The Bureau was in confusion.

A chair had been overturned and the small iron safe stood ajar. It had evidently been rifled, for a cascade of papers poured from its door upon the carpet.

But Congreve did not stop long to inspect that disarray. After a thorough look around, he crossed the room to the door leading out upon the gallery in the *chai*. It was locked with a spring lock and delayed him only a moment. He swung it open, and carrying the tiny flame of the cigar lighter high before him, led the way out upon the gallery. Hastening through the door, we two stood with him upon the very middle of the broad gallery.

Immediately below us there was nothing, but on either side, projecting from beneath the gallery, stood three open vats or hogsheads of polished oak. The long central aisle between the rows of barrels which covered the floor of the *chai* stretched straight away into the darkness. Midway down it the flame of a candle caught our eyes. Silhouetted against its feeble radiance was a dark, hunched figure, moving back and forth, up and down, with grotesque regularity. The man's back was towards us. Our entrance had been quiet and he seemed not to know we had come in.

I don't know whether Congreve was inspired by affection for his friend, the Vicomte, or by sheer love of his wines. At any rate, he showed what seemed an utter lack of caution, and led the way swiftly along the gallery to the staircase. Lewin and I were close at his heels.

We hurried down the staircase as quickly as the poor light permitted. At the foot of the stairs, I found the earthen floor soft and muddy. There was a strong smell of green wine in the air, and I saw with surprise that the vat nearest the staircase had been overturned.

The wet earthen floor made little sound under our feet, and we were soon close upon the intruder, who paid us no heed, but remained muttering and cursing in a low, monotonous tone, as he continued his strange movements.

Congreve suddenly stopped short. "My God," he said.

Lewin and I came up. We three stood abreast, gazing in horror.

Across a barrel in the middle of the aisle, face down, and in the grotesque attitude of death, sprawled the body of a woman in a bedraggled white satin evening dress. The hunched figure held her torso in his hands and appeared to be trying to crush the body against the cask on which it lay. At the sound of Congreve's exclamation, the stooped figure suddenly straightened and turned on us a pale face a face with which his dark eyes, then big with terror, contrasted strangely. At sight of him, Lewin called out in a curious, slow, shocked voice. "Butch, you sot, what have you done?"

At Lewin's words, Butch Marty's hands left the woman's body and shot into his coat pockets.

"I done all that could be done," he said defiantly. "She's dead—murdered. But don't you try to hang it on me. I ain't no more guilty than you are."

Lewin broke in on him. "Shut up, you fool. Pull yourself together and tell us what happened."

"Not me," said Marty. "I ain't sayin' nothin'. Hands off, you guys. I got a gat in my hand. Stand back."

Slowly Marty walked backward away from us, towards the far end of the *chai*. He kept his hands in his pockets. Lewin began cursing and protesting, but to no purpose. Marty had nothing to say.

Meanwhile, Congreve turned to examine the poor woman who lay face down across the barrel. Her identity was already clear to me. It was poor Madame Fürst, her white gown stained and bedraggled, her hair in damp wisps about her dead face. Above the temple, her skull had been crushed in. There was an even round depression there, somewhat larger than a dollar. Her face also showed scars and bruises. She had lost her slippers and was altogether a most pitiful and horrible sight. The body was still warm.

"We'd better get her up into the Bureau," said Congreve. "It's too late for the doctor now. Merton, if you and Lewin can manage to get her upstairs and onto the couch. I want to have a look around here."

Obediently, Lewin and I took up the body and followed Congreve's suggestion. By the time our work was done, and Madame's body decently composed upon the couch in the Bureau, Congreve came up. At the door on the gallery, I heard him call to Marty.

"Well, Butch, coming? Or do you want to be locked in there the rest of the night?"

There was a quick scuffle of feet up the staircase and Butch came into the room, breathing hard.

"Let's get out of here, boss," he said to Lewin. "I've had enough."

Congreve took a cape which hung from a peg in the corner and covered the body. Then he followed us through the door.

"You'd better lock up, Lewin," he said. "I notice the key is still in the outer door."

Closing the door, Lewin fumbled in the darkness, and I heard the rattle of several keys on a key ring. The lock clicked. He turned and brought the key ring into the light.

"Great guns!" he exclaimed, staring at the keys on the palm of his hand. "This is the Vicomte's key ring."

CHAPTER VI
CONGREVE TAKES CHARGE

THE FOUR OF US went back silently into the Château and stood in the *salon*, staring at one another without a word. Lewin seemed to have lost all his usual bounce, to have gone soft and flabby, like a half-inflated toy balloon. He took off his hat carefully and mopped his red face and shining bald head. Marty stood unsteadily, blinking in the soft light like a drunk, bedraggled owl—the whole front of his clothes saturated with wine. As for me, I regretted from the bottom of my heart that I had ever left my comfortable *pension* on the Riviera to get mixed up in a mess like that. Even Congreve, usually so indifferent, had nothing to say.

Lewin was breathing hard and was the first one to find his voice. "This is bad—bad," he kept saying, and nobody seemed to have anything to add to the old gentleman's summary.

It was bad—how bad, none of us guessed even then—bad for poor Madame Fürst, bad for Butch Marty, bad for everybody concerned.

Congreve was the first one to show any initiative or intelligence in these dreadful circumstances.

"Well, gentlemen, I suppose there is only one thing to do now—notify the gendarmes. I suppose all the local police are snoring in their beds at this hour."

I groaned. I could faintly imagine what the next few weeks would be like, after the matter was turned over to the local police. One does not live long in France without acquiring a hearty dislike for the petty officials of its bureaucracy. Congreve went on. "First

50

of all, however, I think we had better have a brandy straight. How about it?" His eyes swept the group.

"You bet," said Marty shakily.

"Excellent idea," was Mr. Lewin's comment, as he laid down his hat.

I said nothing, but followed George over to a table where he was already busy with the decanter and glasses. He poured out stiff ones, and we three tossed them off. Congreve sipped his.

"Hmm," he said appreciatively. "Napoleon brandy."

Then his mind reverted to the problem. "And now for the police. Will you go with me, Merton?"

"Anything you say," I sighed.

"*Bon*," said Congreve. Let's go."

At this moment Lewin came to life. "Just a moment, Mr. Congreve," he begged. "Let's not be hasty in this matter. I can see no point in acting in a hurry. A few minutes, more or less, will make very little difference. I think we should talk this over. After all, you know what Confucius said: 'The wise man acts first and speaks afterward, according to his actions.'"

"But that's what I was going to do—act first, just as Confucius advised."

A bit of a twinkle came into Lewin's tired eyes. "Precisely, but if you read up on Confucius, Mr. Congreve, you will find that he always did a lot of thinking before he began to act. And he did his thinking on rice wine. Another snort of that brandy will put our brains to work. Let's sit down here and go over this business. 'We're in a spot,' as Marty puts it, if I know anything about trouble."

"As you say," said Congreve. "Sit down, everybody. Let's talk."

The three of us moved chairs up to the table, while Congreve brought the tray with the decanter. We all sat down and waited while he poured the brandies.

"Now, gentlemen, my idea is this," said Lewin earnestly. "This business has nothing to do with us, as I see it. But it will be mighty awkward, once the police begin to investigate it. Congreve and Merton, I suppose, are in the clear. But I might have trouble in establishing an alibi for the hour this accident occurred. And Butch here is in it up to the ears. Now, it's my idea that one of us ought to go to work and investigate this thing before the police are informed of it. You boys know France better than I do, of course, but from what little experience I have had and from what I have heard, I gather that once you get involved in the red tape of French officialdom, it takes you a year to get free again. I understand, that by French law, a suspect is held guilty until he can prove himself innocent.

"Now, I've got the money to see us through if we get mixed up with the French courts. It's not the money that bothers me. It's the time. I am getting along. I'm not so young as I was. What I've gone through with is my own funeral, of course, but for years I've been tied down where I couldn't get anything really fit to drink. For a long time, I've planned to take this trip, to make a tour of the French vineyards. If it is humanly possible, I don't intend to be held up. Once the police get on to this, we'll be stuck here for weeks. The vintage will be over and the whole trip shot to hell. It seems to me the least we can do is to try to clear this up to-night. It strikes me that to-morrow morning will be plenty of time to notify the police."

"I suppose you have not considered that if we fail to notify the police, we may be held to have hindered justice and be in deeper than ever," I suggested. But I'm willing to do whatever Congreve thinks is wise. He knows France better than I do."

Lewin turned to me. "That's fine, Mr. Merton. Just what I hoped you'd say. We agree perfectly. Now our friend, Mr. Congreve, has lived in France off and on for years. He knows these people and their ways. He can parlevoo with any of them. What's more, they know him and respect him. He has influential friends here. Whatever he says goes, with me. I'll back him to the limit. If he'll undertake this investigation and try to find out what's at the bottom of this, there's some hope of our getting clear and going on our way rejoicing. And that is my idea of what ought to be done."

Congreve's face expressed astonishment and disapproval at Lewin's suggestion. He smiled sardonically and slowly shook his head. I expected a flat negative from him.

But Lewin was before him. The old gentleman raised his hand to stop Congreve's denial of his plea.

"Now don't be hasty, Mr. Congreve. Let's take our time. This is a serious matter. You're not guilty. You've got an alibi in Mr. Merton here. The two of you stand clear, but how about the rest of us—me and Butch and the girls? You can't pull out and leave us flat. I don't think you're that kind."

"Thanks for your flattering opinion on such short acquaintance," said Congreve. "But I—"

"Just a moment, Mr. Congreve," Lewin went on earnestly. "I know you're no detective, but you can solve this thing if you try, I feel sure. We are guests in this house. Its a question whether we have any right to take things into our own hands and notify the police before our host gets back from Bordeaux. After all, this is his place. He's in charge. I don't think we ought to move in the matter until we see him again."

Congreve made no reply. He sat with one forearm on the table, twisting his glass between thumb and forefinger round and round. The three of us sat motionless. The silence was oppressive.

Finally, he leaned back in his chair and smiled. There was always something comforting in George Congreve's smile.

"I suppose we ought to consult Monkhouse," he said. "I understand he is the Vicomte's nephew."

Lewin jumped at that suggestion.

"That's fair enough," he agreed. "But we must remember that Monkhouse is an alien too. He's a guest here, the same as ourselves, and if it comes to a showdown, he must take his chance like everybody else. From what I've seen of that Englishman, I should think he'd be glad to have us take the responsibility, but if you want to call him in, it's all right with me. All I propose is that you undertake this investigation and go ahead with it until the Vicomte turns up."

"Very well, Lewin. I'll undertake the investigation," Congreve said.

Lewin rose from his chair, reached across the table and clasped Congreve's hand, giving it a hearty shake.

"That's fine, Mr. Congreve. I knew you wouldn't let me down."

"But on three conditions," Congreve continued. "First, that I carry on only until the Vicomte shows up. After that, it is up to him."

"Fair enough," cried Lewin, thoroughly pleased.

"Second," said Congreve, "that we send word to the Vicomte to return at once. We can probably get word to him in Bordeaux and have him back within three or four hours at most."

"Excellent," said Lewin. "That's damn clever. That ought to put us in the clear with the police until he gets back. Nothing could be fairer than that."

Congreve, plump and deliberate as always, glanced quizzically at Lewin.

"The third condition is that I have the key to the wine cellar."

We all looked our astonishment.

"Why in the world do you say that, Mr. Congreve? What do you want the key to the wine cellar for?"

"I should think that is perfectly obvious. Why should any one want the key to the wine cellar?— To get something to drink, of course," he explained.

We all stared in silence at the apparent frivolity of this demand.

"I'm afraid I don't get you, Mr. Congreve," said Lewin, his serious face growing slowly red with chagrin. "I should think you'd want all your wits about you at a time like this. Surely there are enough bottles on the sideboard in the dining room to satisfy any ordinary taste. There'll be time enough for drinking when we're out of this terrible difficulty."

George Congreve shook his head sadly at what he evidently considered Lewin's stupidity.

"My dear fellow," he made answer. "There are plenty of bottles, but not the *right* bottles. You and the Vicomte selected them. I prefer to choose my own."

Still we stared in silence as Lewin's heavy face settled into sullen lines of disapproval.

"This is no time for monkeyshines, sir," he said. "It is all very well to make a study of vintages a lifetime hobby, but to spend a night like this exploring the bins of a wine cellar, with such a pressing problem to be solved strikes me as being nothing short of indecent. I thought better of you, sir. I swear I did."

Congreve sighed.

"You don't understand, Lewin. Even Merton seems to be mystified. Of course, Marty would be. All my life I have made a study of the fine points of wines—mostly French wines. With you, drinking is merely a pleasure. With me, it is an art. You rejoice at a new flavor, a new bouquet. Merton enjoys the exaltation induced by a good bottle, and Marty, poor sot, drinks only for the kick he gets from alcohol. You are all barbarians—if you will pardon the characterization. Not that I have anything to say against pleasure, against the pleasant glow induced by wine, but you don't understand and so I pardon you."

None of us enjoyed his description of us as barbarians. I was distinctly annoyed. Marty glared at him, while Lewin choked with fury.

Congreve, however, went calmly on explaining his position.

"You have done me the honor of believing that I have a considerable knowledge of wines. I know you believe, because you have been willing to pay for a share of that knowledge. You must, therefore, bear with me while I explain how that knowledge may serve us all in this predicament. Wine, my dear fellow, produces far more than a mere physical effect. It is much more than a pleasant smell, a pleasant flavor, a pleasant glow. Wine does things to the brain and spirit. The right bottle puts the soul of man *en rapport* with the external world. There is hardly any state of mind which cannot be induced by a glass or two of the proper vintage. In ordinary life, these states of mind come of themselves. One day we feel gay, lighthearted; another day serious, another quick-witted; but such states of mind cannot be experienced by water drinkers in rapid succession or at will. You have asked me to solve a difficult problem, of which I, as yet, know next to nothing, all within a few hours. Yet you are annoyed when I propose that you give me the key to the only means I have of inducing the various states of mind which may permit me to solve the various intricacies as they may arise. I confess I am hurt that you thought I would take advantage of you at such a time in order to gratify my pleasure in drinking from the best bins of the Château. But in this emergency, I suppose I must overlook that. It is my experience and my conviction that with the aid of the right bottle, a man can solve any problem which human wit can solve, once he understands the nature of it. I have the knowledge which enables me to choose the right bottle. Therefore, I want the key to that cellar. If that seems too much to ask, go ahead and handle the thing in your own way. I'll be no party to it."

For a long moment, there was utter silence, while we absorbed the lesson he had read us. Marty probably was uncertain whether Congreve was in earnest or not. I knew him too well to doubt it. And Lewin, after studying Congreve's face and giving a quick glance at mine, reached impulsively into his pocket and flung down a great iron key upon the table.

"Mr. Congreve, I beg your pardon. I had forgotten that your palate has a memory."

PART TWO
THE EVIDENCE

CHAPTER I
THE EVIDENCE OF THE BODYGUARD

As the metal rang upon the dark wood of the table, a look of surprise came into Congreve's face—a look perhaps of suspicion, as it seemed to me. I don't know what Marty was thinking—if the poor sobered sot thought at all at that moment. But for my part, I was astonished.

Congreve was first to break the silence. "Well, Lewin," he said, "I hardly expected such a prompt fulfillment of my third condition. I supposed we should have to talk Monkhouse and the *maître de chai* into letting us have the key temporarily. May I ask where you got it?"

Lewin appeared uncomfortable. His face flushed slightly and his eyes fell to the glass of brandy in his hand. For a moment he hesitated. Then he looked up and smiled with an unconvincing air.

"Well, Mr. Congreve, now that you're the official investigator, I guess we must keep no secrets from you. So I will tell you gentlemen in confidence that the Vicomte left the key in my hands when he went off to Bordeaux this afternoon. You know that one of my main objects in making this trip was to acquire a cellar to take back home. So while I was in the cave with him, we made a sort of tentative deal—that is to say, conditional on your approval, Mr. Congreve. He left the key with me so that you might inspect the bins at your leisure. Of course, I couldn't make it final without your advice. You know how much I value that, of course. But when I got down into that wonderful cellar surrounded by those thousands of bottles of choice wines—well, I guess I lost my head a little. At any rate, there's the key."

Lewin looked as sheepish as if he had been a boy caught stealing apples. Congreve pocketed the key.

"Splendid, Lewin. I foresee that your tour of the vineyards will keep me hopping. Unless I look out, you'll buy up all the bottles in France without giving me a chance to earn my pay."

He rose from the table.

"The next thing we must do is consult Monkhouse and gain his approval of the delay."

Lewin tossed off his brandy and rose to his feet more actively than I would have believed possible in a man of his years and bulk. His eyes were shining. All his natural liveliness had come back to him.

"Okay, Sherlock," he agreed. "I suppose Monkhouse is in the dining room."

I got to my feet also and prepared to follow Lewin. Then I noticed that Congreve's brandy stood untouched on the table.

"Aren't you forgetting your drink, George?" I asked.

Congreve looked down at the brandy as though reluctant to leave it.

"Thanks, Merton," he said. "You're right. I mustn't waste that."

He took up the glass and, with a sigh, carefully poured it back into the decanter. Seeing my astonishment, he added, "I don't think brandy is what's wanted just now."

I looked up and saw Marty stealing from the room. Congreve paid no attention, but Lewin saw the man's sneaking figure and whirled on him. His voice was sharp with anger.

"Butch, come back here. You can't sneak out on me."

Butch stopped, his ugly face fiercely stubborn, and jammed his hand into his coat pocket.

"The hell I can't. Watch me," he said. "You can't pin this on me. If you think I'll take a rap for you, you're crazy. Stand where you are. Keep back. I'll plug you if you move."

The hand in his pocket was thrust forward, his attitude was menacing, deadly.

Then Lewin showed a courage which I would not have expected from such a lover of pleasure. "Butch, you fool," he growled.

In two steps, he was beside the man and had caught his arm.

"Lay off me. I'll shoot, Mr. Lewin," Butch shouted.

But Lewin paid no heed. "Shoot your belly full, you poor sot." He swung Butch round.

There was a deafening roar as the gun exploded. A jet of flame leapt towards a great mirror on the wall opposite. In the silence which followed, Lewin laughed.

"You're a hell of a bodyguard, Butch," he taunted. "It's lucky for you I loaded that gun with blanks. If you had busted that mirror, you would have had seven years' bad luck."

Butch jerked his arm free, bewildered, then yanked the gun out of his pocket. He released the magazine of the Colt automatic and inspected the cartridges in it. Then with an oath, he flung the gun down on the nearest chair and crouched as though to spring on his employer.

"You tricked me, damn you," he yelled, beside himself. "But I'll not go to Devil's Island for you. You can't hang it on me that easy."

Lewin's voice was impatient.

"Snap out of it, Butch,—" he commanded. "You've had too much to drink. You're always half-shot. That's why I loaded your gun with blanks. Nobody wants to drink opposite a dumb sot with a loaded Colt in his pocket. You're dumber than I thought you were— If you think I would try to frame you. What would Mamma say to that?"

At the mention of Mrs. Lewin, Butch froze in his tracks. Within a few seconds, a complete change was evident in his attitude and in his eyes. His muscles relaxed. His eyes fell. He was once more the obedient hireling.

"Okay, Mr. Lewin," he muttered. "Let's go." He picked up the gun.

By this time, the door leading into the dining room had opened a crack, and the timid eye of a servant peered through. As we approached the door, it closed again. When Lewin attempted to open the door, he found that some one on the other side was holding it shut. He could not turn the handle.

"Come on, Butch," he said. "You've scared that Frog to death."

Butch came forward obediently, seized the handle, and with a mighty wrench turned it, jerking the door wide. The servant fell over himself getting clear of the opening and disappeared through the door opposite. We all crowded forward into the dining room.

Monkhouse sat at table with a cup of coffee before him.

"Hello," he said good-humoredly, "I thought you had all deserted me. What's going on—target practice in the *salon?* I fancy the Vicomte won't approve that, you know."

"It's worse than that, Mr. Monkhouse," Lewin broke out excitedly.

Congreve interrupted. "Perhaps I had better do the talking, Lewin. You see, Monkhouse, I have something to tell you—something important."

"Aoh," said the Englishman, "I hope it is not a long story."

"I'm afraid it may be," Congreve admitted.

"Then, if you don't mind, I'll buzz up to my room and get a pipe," Monkhouse announced. "I can't listen properly without my pipe, you know. I sha'n't be a moment."

He got to his feet and started off. At the door he paused.

"By the by, Lewin, I brought the Scotch for your man. There it is on the table."

Two bottles stood together near Marty's plate. "Cheerio," said Monkhouse. And in a moment, Congreve had closed the door behind him.

After the Englishman had gone, we dropped into our chairs again.

"Now what, Mr. Congreve?" Lewin asked anxiously. "If you're all set, let's go."

"I suppose the first thing is to get Marty's story," Congreve directed. "If he'll talk."

Marty scowled suspiciously at Congreve.

"You can't make me talk," he grumbled. "I can't see what good talking will do, anyhow. You're wasting your time picking on me. Catch the guys that done it."

Lewin broke in angrily. "Butch, listen to me. I'm your boss and you'll talk if I say talk. Well, I do say it. What's more, I'm your friend. If you're guilty of any crime, I'll stand by you. If you're not, you'll be doing yourself no good by keeping silence. That's hindering justice. Mr. Congreve will ask you questions and you're going to answer them. Don't forget that."

"Aw, who's he to put the screws on me?" Butch flared up. "He ain't no detective."

Lewin laid his hand on Butch's shoulder. "No, he's no detective, thank God. That's why you're going to answer his questions here and now as a free man, instead of talking to a lot of Frog cops in a cell. Snap out of it. We have no time to lose."

"You can't expect me to incriminate myself," Butch defended his stand.

Lewin shook the man's shoulder impatiently.

"You're in it now up to your ears, you fool. Come clean. You broke into the *chai* and stole wine, contrary to my orders. Burglary is bad enough. If you hide what you know, you'll be held for murder too, more than likely. Come clean. Make it snappy."

"Okay, Mr. Lewin," Butch grumbled, and looked sullenly at Congreve. "Shoot," he added.

"All I want to know," said Congreve, "is just what happened after you left us."

Butch shifted uneasily on his chair, licked his lips, and began. "Okay. Well, you know how it was. I had been drinking and I wanted to keep my buzz. Mr. Lewin here said I'd had enough, so I got mad and went out to get somethin' to drink. At first, I thought I'd go to the village and buy a drink, but it was pretty late. Then I remembered that I didn't have no money. Mr. Lewin here won't let me carry none, cause he says I'd spend it all on booze. Well, I knew that Frog barkeep wouldn't trust me a stranger and tight as I was. Besides, a cold wind was coming up, and it was a mile's walk to town. Anyhow, I could see the gates were shut and maybe locked.

"So then I thought I'd go and bust into the cellar and help myself. But then stealing wine from a cellar is tricky business in France. When I was over here in the War, I knew some fellows who got into a hell of a lot of trouble playing tricks like that. Anyhow, I went over to the cellar door and fooled around for a while, looking into the window. But there was all them servants inside, wide awake and talking. So I figured they'd hear any noise I'd make that close, and give it up. Well, there was only one other place where I could expect to find wine in this here Château. That was where they keep the barrels."

"You mean the *chai*," Lewin interrupted.

"Yeah. That big barn where the barrels is—where the Count took us this afternoon. Well, it was the Count hisself that give me the tip. Remember, he pointed out a hole in the ceiling, and told how the Yanks, billeted up in the loft, had cut that hole and clumb down a rope every night to help theirselves to his liquor? He told us all about that. Said it wasn't the first time Americans had tasted his wine."

"I don't remember anything of the kind," said Congreve.

"Aw, that was when you went out to meet your friend, Mr. Merton, here, I guess. Anyhow, he told us all about it and how there was a staircase leading up to the loft. So I drifted over to that side of the place and begun to look for that stair. Well, I come under the archway where the drive is, and sure enough, there was a stair-case going up the wall from the door of the Count's office. So I slipped up there, but couldn't find no door into the loft. There was only one door and it went into a room with a light in it."

Congreve broke in, "You mean the Englishman's rooms, I suppose."

Marty nodded. "Yeah. That's it. Well, I didn't want to bust in there, so I slipped downstairs again and went on through the drive into the vineyard, and followed along the wall of the building on that side. Sure enough, I come spang against an outside staircase going up. Well, it didn't take me long to get to the top of that and find a door. It wasn't locked, so I lifted the latch and swung it open, easy-like, and stuck my head in to listen.

"For a while I couldn't hear nothing. Then I sensed a kind of a thumpin' sound—not very loud. But it seemed to come from a distance; so after a while, I slipped in, shut the door easy, and struck a match. That loft up there ain't very high, but it's big and empty. I couldn't hear nothing but the wind over the roof and a thumpin' that sounded like it might be anywhere. But I couldn't see nobody. There was nobody there.

"So I begun to look for that hole the Yanks had made. I knew I could find it, 'cause I saw from downstairs yesterday that it was covered with wide planks. It was close to the wall, so all I had to do was to watch my step and move along the wall till I come to them wide planks.

"Well, I kept going and kept going till I got clear to the end of the goddam loft and never found it. That sure had me stumped for a while. And finally I figured it must be on the other side of the door I come in at, so I turned around and followed the wall back past the door and on clean up to the corner. And sure enough, there was the wide planks. I could still hear that thumpin', and it seemed louder now, so I kept mighty quiet, cause I didn't know where it was coming from or whether it was the wind or somebody in the building.

"I got down on my knees alongside them planks and lit a match and looked them over, 'cause I didn't want to make no noise. Well, everything looked fine. The planks was nailed together to make a kind of door or lid to the hole, about three feet square. And lucky for me, it wasn't nailed down. Anyhow, I thought it was lucky for me then. I ain't so sure now.

"I forgot to tell you that I had found a piece of rope in the loft and figured I'd let myself down on that. Yesterday I remembered seeing a key in the lock of that little door into the vineyard, so I figured I wouldn't have to climb the rope again, anyhow. Well, I lifted up the lid, easy-like, and propped it back against the wall, tied the rope around a post there, and was all set to slide down. I done this in the dark, you see, 'cause I couldn't manage to tie the rope and hold a lighted match at the same time. Well, when I got the rope tied and the lid up, I stuck my head down. Then I seen there was a light downstairs under the gallery. The gallery is about six feet wide. It runs clear across the end of the room. Under that was where the light was—not a big light, just like a candle might be. And then I heard the thumpin' begin again. Not very loud, but louder than it seemed before.

"Then it stops, and I seen somebody come out from under the gallery. At first I thought it was a woman in a blue dress. Then I seen that it was somebody in one of them long blue coats the Frogs use for overalls."

"You mean a workman's blouse?" Congreve suggested.

"Yeah. That's it, I reckon. So I thought it must be a man. Then it come to my mind that if I could see him, more than likely he could see me, if he looked up. So I eased back away from the hole and laid low for a while. He kept fussing around down there, and I could hear a little noise now and then, but not much. I don't know how long I waited, but pretty soon I stuck my head out again, and whoever was down there was out of sight under the gallery again.

"About that time, the door into the office opened, and a woman come out on the gallery. It was this Madame. I knew her by her white dress and her funny voice. She was talking kind of low. Seemed like she was calling somebody. Well, the minute she be-gun to squawk, the light under the gallery went out. And there we all was in the dark. She kept calling, 'Daniel, oh, Daniel!'

"Then this Madame strikes a light and comes clicking down the steps in her high heels to the main floor. She went under the gal-lery. Then they both began to jabber in some foreign lingo. I couldn't tell what they were saying. They didn't talk loud, but kept jabbering faster and faster all the time. Sometimes her match would go out and they'd be in the dark. And then again, one of them would light up while the talk went on. They was three of them, the woman, the man in the blue coat, and somebody else.

"By this time I was getting interested and kept watching all the time. I figured they was too busy to be looking for me. And I was drunk and careless. Anyhow, I kept looking down. Most of the time, I could hear just two voices. Then all at once, I heard the third one—high and squeaky—speaking English it was. Just one thing. That was the only thing I could make out clear through the whole business."

"What was that?" Congreve demanded.

We all listened anxiously for Marty's reply.

"Well, it don't hardly make sense, but he said it twice, so I'm sure I got it right. The two of them talked low, like I said, but this fellow—high and squeaky—was yelling 'Daniel dunno Percy—Daniel dunno Percy!' That's what I heard—plain English—excited-like.

"Well, right after that, this Madame rushed out from under the gallery, like she was crazy, down to where the end of the row of barrels is at the foot of the stairs. She turned sharp there to get up the stairs, and down she went. I guess them high heels ain't made to run in. Anyhow, she slipped there and fell down, making the turn. And by the time she got to her feet, a guy in a black coat was right after her. She run up the stairs as if her life depended on it, and him right after her, with the candle in one hand. He ran so fast the candle mighty near went out and I couldn't see very well. So I eased forward to stick my head down farther.

"Well, I guess I must have touched that goddam lid when I moved. Anyhow, down it come with a hell of a bang onto the floor. Before I could jerk back out of sight, they was both at the top of the stairs, and stopped like they was shot. When they stopped, it seemed like the candle got brighter again.

"The one in the black coat had his back to me. All I could see was his coat and his black head. It all happened in a split second. He up with a mallet and socked her one on the bean. Then the light went out.

"I laid there, scared to death. Then I heard somebody running on the stairs and the office door banged shut. Right after that, I heard somebody scuttling down the main floor between the barrels. Right away, I heard the little door to the vineyard creaking open and shut again.

"Well, I didn't know what to think for a minute and laid there as still as a mouse. I thought maybe that guy, whoever he was, had bumped her off, and they had both run out. If I had had any sense, I would have got out of there the way I come. But pretty soon, I heard the door to the office bang shut again, so I figured she'd cleared out that way.

"Well, after what seemed about an hour, I made up my mind to get down the rope, 'cause I sure needed a drink. The gallery was right underneath the hole where I was. It wasn't much of a drop, so I slid down the rope all right, and felt along the handrail of the gallery till I come to the stairs and eased my way down to the floor. The Madame was gone. There wasn't a sound, and I fumbled around, trying to find a loose bung, but they was all hammered in tight, so's I couldn't do nothing with my bare hands. I didn't much want to strike a light, but I was sure the back door was open to the vineyard, 'cause one of these guys had run out that way. So I took a chance and looked around for a hammer where they make the barrels. It didn't take me long to find one, and I started to pick out a barrel to get a drink.

"I remembered the Count said the best wine was at the far end of the room, so I come out from under the gallery and started down that way, holding a match high to see my way. Well, then I seen her two legs sticking out of the hogshead beside the stair—two legs with silk stockings, one of them with a muddy slipper on.

"Well, that give me a shock, you bet.

"I didn't know how she got there, but I knew damn well she must be drowning. So I drops the match and tried to get her out. Well, I was pretty drunk, I guess, and them hogsheads are deep, and she wasn't no lightweight either. I heaved and pulled, but I couldn't hist her over the edge of that barrel. I didn't know what to do.

"Then I figured that if I could turn the damned thing over with her in it, I could get her out that way. But the barrel was too heavy for me. I pushed and pulled my damnedest, but I couldn't budge it.

"Then I thought the only way to save her was to smash the barrel in and let the wine out. Then maybe, I figured, I could turn it over and give her first aid. Well, the hammer wasn't very big, but I kept slugging away till I busted the barrel a little and knocked out the spigot. The wine come pouring out in the dark and soaked me all over. And pretty soon, I could turn the thing over, and she come sloshing out all over the ground. So I dragged her onto a barrel, face down, and pumped the wine out of her lungs and tried to bring her to."

Marty's face was working with excitement. His voice became shrill.

"God damn it! She wouldn't come to. So I quit working with her for a minute and looked around for that candle. Well, I found it after a while and lighted it, but when I seen her, all slimy, with her head bashed in, I got cold feet all at once. I thought, 'Here you are, you poor devil, with this murdered woman on your hands. They'll find you and hang it on you.'"

"Well, what did you do?" said Congreve.

"Hell's bells, Mr. Congreve, I ain't no hero, I guess. I beat it down between them barrels to the back door to make my getaway. But would you believe it? The goddam skunk had took the key and locked the door on the outside. There I was—caught like a rat in a trap. I run up the stairs to the door on the gallery. It was locked too. So I tried to shin up the rope again, but I couldn't make it. It was too far, and I was too shaky or something. So I went back again and went to work, like you found me. And that's the God's truth."

CHAPTER II
BOUQUET

MARTY SAT WITH his clenched fists on the table, his face strained with anxiety, watching Congreve.

Congreve sat quiet and easy, and when he saw that Marty had finished, his intent gaze relaxed.

"You have nothing to add, Marty?" he asked.

"No, sir. That's all I can think of now," the man replied.

"Very well," Congreve answered, getting to his feet. "Run along into the other room and take it easy for a while. You'll find the brandy in the small decanter rather good—Napoleon brandy it is, if I'm not mistaken."

"You bet, Mr. Congreve."

Marty was on his feet and out of the room in a jiffy.

"You make a mistake giving your bodyguard Scotch, Lewin," said Congreve. "And good wine is wasted on him. You'll find him a far more interesting companion if you restrict him to brandy. I remember a bottle—"

Lewin banged the table with his fist. "Oh, for Heaven's sake, Congreve, never mind the bottles now. What do you say to Butch's story?"

Congreve stared.

"Very interesting," he said dryly, drifting over to the buffet covered with the dusty bottles brought from the Vicomte's cellar. "Good story."

"Too good," was Lewin's comment. "He saw too much—and too little."

Congreve was inspecting the moldy labels of the bottles on the buffet. Presently he came back, bringing one of them. He removed the capsule and drew out the cork, then gently poured a little into his glass, and having sniffed it, nodded his head approvingly and served us each half a glass in turn. With a contented sigh, he sank into his chair, and cupping the glass in his two hands, warmed it so.

"Too bad we haven't more time, gentlemen," he said cryptically.

Lewin stared. Then with a sigh, he evidently decided to humor Congreve. Raising his glass, he sipped it.

"My dear fellow," Congreve said. "One doesn't drink a fine old Burgundy at the temperature of the cellar. Warm it, man, warm it. Cuddle it. Bring it to the temperature of the room. I grant you that this room is only a few degrees warmer than the cellar to-night, but one must do what one can. You will lose all the bouquet. And this is really a magnificent old Burgundy."

Lewin broke out. "Come now, Mr. Congreve. No more of this fooling. Let's get down to the facts. We have no time to lose. If you can't think without drinking, drink your wine, damn it. And let's get to work."

Congreve groaned a bit impatiently at Lewin and shook his head.

"The trouble with you, Lewin, is haste, impatience. I'm afraid you'll never make a true connoisseur. The more haste, the less taste. When I say I must go at this in my own way, I mean it. This is my approach to life, as well as to wine. You think the bouquet is of little importance, but you make a great mistake there. The bouquet, the flavor, comes first and is most significant. And so with what happened to-night. But you want everything explained in brutal detail."

"Facts are stubborn things, Mr. Congreve," Lewin countered.

"Precisely. And we have the facts, if we only give them time to reveal their savor, their significance. A hint to the wise is sufficient. It isn't necessary to swallow a whole bottle at a gulp in order to appreciate it. And so with the murder to-night. Give it time. Warm it in your brain. Warm Butch's story in your brain. Perhaps it will reveal its meaning better so."

"I don't know what you mean," Lewin grumbled. "If we only knew a little more—"

"Let's make the most of what we *do* know, first. There will be plenty of facts later. The significance is what we're after. What do *these* facts mean?"

"Well," Lewin blurted out, "what *do* they mean?"

Congreve considered gravely, his nose in his glass, his eyes closed.

"One thing strikes me very forcibly, Lewin. It's the similarity of character between our friend, Marty, and poor Madame Fürst."

Lewin snorted. "I don't see it. Utterly different in every respect, in my opinion."

"Oh, Lewin, Lewin," Congreve objected. "What a dull life you must have lived. I suppose you think that a man's character—or shall we say a woman's—is best displayed by that person's action in a great crisis, where some far-reaching choice is to be made. But in that I think you are mistaken. Consider the method of a great novelist. It is only a second-rate novelist who has to shove his hero into such a crisis in order to display his character. A man's real self is constantly betrayed in the smallest actions. Any one with a seeing eye will understand a man's character from these. Significant trifles, my dear fellow, *those* are the key to character, and character is the key to destiny. Why was Madame Fürst murdered? Why did Butch happen to see it done? For the same reason, obviously. Both of them are insubordinate, greedy, persistent creatures who, in spite of the plainest warnings, keep on going after what they want."

"For example—" Lewin growled.

"For example, Butch wants alcohol. You refuse it. He goes after it. And even the sight of a murder committed before his eyes does not deter him from his quest. Madame Fürst also obviously came into the *chai* looking for something—"

"For Daniel," Lewin broke in.

"Yes," Congreve agreed, "or for something Daniel could give her. Now the question arises—why does an unmarried woman, so amiable, so well-dressed, so expensive, consort with well-to-do cosmopolites? The answer is plain. If we had never seen Madame Fürst, the answer would be plain. As the French say, *elle cherche*."

"You mean she's a gold digger?" Lewin demanded. "Somebody's mistress?"

"What else could she be, under the circumstances?" I threw in.

Congreve nodded. "If, then, she came looking for Daniel, you may assume with some certainty that Daniel was a catch for her. Why should she go looking in such unlikely places for Daniel except for her own advantage? Obviously Daniel was in the nature of a prize for her. He had something she wanted—something she was determined to get. Otherwise, she would never have gone into the *chai* in the dark, calling his name."

"That *was* funny," said Lewin. "For her to go into that dirty place dressed up fit to kill at that time of night was queer, and no mistake."

"Funny—and bold," Congreve agreed. "Why should she suppose he was in there in the first place? And then consider what happened when she called his name. He immediately put out the light."

"Maybe the wind blew the light out when she opened the door," I suggested.

"It may be," Congreve said. "But the candle—I suppose it was a candle—was under the gallery. It would hardly go out so easily. One of them ran up the stairs with it later and it didn't go out. One of them must have put it out."

"Evidently Daniel didn't want her to see *him* there—if it *was* Daniel," Lewin threw in. "But we've got to remember that Marty was drunk and scared. Therefore I don't put too much faith in his story."

"Could he have made it all up?" I asked. "It seemed to hang together. He hardly had time to frame such a story. He couldn't have been in there long."

"Let's see. It was nine-fifty when he pulled out. I remember I looked at my watch then and thought how late it was. It must have been all of fifteen minutes before I went looking for him. What time was it when we found him with the body?" Lewin asked.

"Past the half-hour," I offered. "I remember hearing the chimes of the village church while we were in the courtyard."

"We found him at ten-forty precisely," Congreve stated. "I looked at my watch. He couldn't have been with her much more than twenty minutes at the outside."

"Hmm," said Lewin. "But who's Percy? That's what I want to know. 'Daniel don't know Percy' was what one of them said, and in English too. The two of them kept jabbering in French, I guess, but one of them talked English—high and squeaky voice, and 'excited-like.' Now, when a man's excited, he generally talks in the language that comes most natural the language that he was brought up on."

"Good for you, Lewin," said Congreve. "Trifles like that are always most significant."

I objected. "But these Continentals speak so many languages, I doubt if that means anything. Anyhow, we don't know who Daniel or who Percy is. Until we find that out, I can't see that we've got anywhere. Even then we don't know that she found Daniel under the gallery. The question is—who hit her with the mallet? Butch said he wore a black coat and had black hair."

"Did he?" asked Congreve.

"That's what I understood," said Lewin. "It could only be this guy, Arno, in that case. He has a black coat and black hair. He socked her over the head, shoved her in the vat, and beat it. The other guy got cold feet then and beat it by the other door."

"Ah, yes," said Congreve. "The two doors. And footsteps on the stairs in the dark—that's difficult."

"And then the third door banged," Lewin rushed on. "You remember, we heard that ourselves—the outer door of the office. He waited there till the coast was clear, then ducked out, ran into the vineyard, or maybe skipped upstairs to the Englishman's room. He couldn't have come into the courtyard. We'd have seen him."

Congreve put in his oar. "Odd that he should have banged *both* doors after him."

"Not so very," Lewin objected. "The man was scared."

Congreve frowned.

"He might have banged one door in his excitement, but hardly two. The second time, he would be more careful, especially as it was an outside door. You note that the man who went out the back door made very little noise—no banging."

"Butch heard the three doors close and thought all three of them had gone. But who ran up the stairs?"

"Maybe there were four of them," I suggested.

"The murderer was already at the top of the stairs when the light went out," Lewin said. "The second man may have run upstairs after him. The third one went out the back way into the vineyard."

"Quite a convention of murderers, like an old play—*first, second, and third murderers exeunt by several doors*," said Congreve. "But I'm afraid that hardly holds water. First of all, Butch heard the door on the gallery bang shut. It has a spring lock. He couldn't open it. If the murderer banged that door shut, how could the second man get through it when he ran up the stairs?"

"Maybe he had a key," Lewin offered.

"Maybe," Congreve agreed reluctantly. "But it was odd Butch didn't hear the door open. He must have been all ears at that moment."

"He didn't hear the man throw the body into the vat," was my comment.

"Quite so," said Congreve. "And the question arises— *Did* the man throw the body into the vat? From that height, it must have made a considerable splash, but Marty said nothing of such a sound. Yet there in the vat the body was, or so he said. It was not on the gallery or on the staircase when he went down, that's certain."

"Well," I suggested, I suppose the next thing is to identify Daniel and Percy. Don't you think so, Congreve?"

Congreve's eyes were dreamy again, and he came out of his reverie with a start.

"Oh, yes," he said. "We must know that sooner or later, but isn't it odd about that muddy slipper? And there's another point. Madame fell as she turned to run up the stairs."

"High heels," Lewin threw in. "Butch said it was her high heels, you remember."

"So he did," Congreve nodded. "That is what's so odd about it. She was running, you remember, running her fastest, running for her life. Her strides couldn't have been long in that clinging gown. She must have been running on her toes. That will require consideration."

"I think," he added, "we'd better send for the *maître de chai*."

CHAPTER III
THE EVIDENCE OF THE *MAÎTRE DE CHAI*

THE *MAÎTRE DE CHAI* entered, methodically closed the door behind him, and stood facing us, blinking a little against the lights. There was an air of solidity about the burly Gascon's steady figure, and face topped off by a shock of white hair—an air of responsibility, of a strong sense of personal identity. He was a hale, hearty old fellow.

Congreve made him welcome.

"Come in, Jules," he said, in French. "Seat yourself. A serious accident has happened to-night, which may concern you. Your master is absent. I am trying to find out everything possible, so that the information may be placed before him immediately on his return. I need your help. Please sit down."

"At your service, Monsieur."

Congreve brought a bottle from the buffet. "For this conference, I think a manly wine is indicated. Suppose we open this red Hermitage." He scanned the label with obvious appreciation. "Les Baumes, 1920," he murmured, in a tone of keen anticipation. "A good year for that vintage, Jules. You approve?"

"The greatest of the century, they say, Monsieur," he answered.

It was clear that such a treat was unusual. But I thought the old man seemed uneasy at the prospect of consuming such a "grand bottle" in his master's absence.

"*Bon*," said Congreve.

When the bottle was open and we had all been served, he took his seat opposite Jules.

"Presently I shall ask you to drink to my success in this investigation. But now I must question you. I suppose you keep the cellar book of the Château?"

Jules nodded.

"Excellent," said Congreve. "I shall want that. When we have finished here, please bring it to me. You are to understand that your master, the Vicomte, has entered into an agreement with this gentleman, M. Lewin, to part with a portion of his cellar. Mr. Lewin has requested me to make the se lections. Of course, I could search the bins, but time presses. Moreover," he said, with a smile, "I suspect you would prefer not to have strangers fingering your precious bottles more than is absolutely necessary."

Jules relaxed a little.

"You are right, Monsieur," he replied. "This turning over the key to a stranger—it is without precedent. I will bring you the book at once."

"Very well," said Congreve. "We also have decided that it would be best to send immediately for your master, the Vicomte. This accident to-night is very serious. He should be informed at once. Can you suggest any way of reaching him? Do you know where he went?"

This suggestion was evidently pleasing to Jules, and he hastened to explain that the Vicomte had gone to Bordeaux to see the notary on business. He said he was sure of the route his master would follow. It would be only a matter of sending some one in a car to the notary's house in Bordeaux. There was a car for hire in the village. Or it might be, he said, that the Englishman's car could be used. After all, the Englishman was M. le Vicomte's nephew. The *maître* was certain the matter could be arranged speedily.

"Excellent," was Congreve's comment. "And now there is another matter. It is necessary to question the servants of the Château—to determine how each one spent his time from the hour of nine until eleven o'clock. You know these people and should be able to get the truth from them. My friend, M. Merton, here, will gladly assist you."

Jules was evidently relieved at the way things were going, though he kept up an air of puzzlement. He assured Congreve that nothing could be simpler. As for the servants, he thought they had nearly all been together after dinner. He could readily ascertain what each of them had been doing, he said.

"And now," said Congreve, "fortify yourself, my friend, with a glass of this excellent wine. We come now to the point. This accident to-night is very serious. It occurred in the *chai*."

Jules seemed startled and half rose to his feet, but Congreve's eye upon him steadied him, and he sat down again.

"In the *chai?*" he muttered. "Impossible!"

Briefly Congreve explained the nature of the accident and what was known of it. As the facts fell one by one from his lips, the Gascon became more and more excited.

"But this was murder—not accident!" he declared.

"Precisely. What can you tell us about it?"

Jules' heavy face flushed, his eyes glittered, his fists clenched about the stem of his glass. The old man spoke with suppressed fury.

"You accuse me—*me*," he demanded, "of this murder?"

"I accuse nobody," Congreve replied. "But until the truth is known, every one in the Château is suspect. After all, I know very little as yet. One of the men seen in the *chai* with the murdered woman was wearing a blue blouse. There is reason to believe that the garment belonged to you, Jules. At any rate, the blouse found under the gallery was yours. It was easily recognized by the stains upon it. You remember you had it on all the afternoon."

"Yes, I remember. No doubt the blouse is mine," he replied, calmer now. "You identified the cap too, I suppose?"

"No, not the cap," Congreve admitted. "We did not find the cap."

The *maître* caught at this straw. "But it must be there still. I left it there along with the blouse. You see, Messieurs, to-night my head is bare. Regard also how my hair is white. It does not correspond to the description of the man who struck down Madame."

"Do not forget the man under the gallery," Lewin suggested, in English.

Instantly Jules turned on him.

"*Comment?*" he cried.

Congreve explained what Lewin had said. "Marty says there were two of them, at least."

"I know nothing about it. Nothing," Jules declared. "I locked the *chai* when we left it. I made sure that *all* the doors were locked."

"And the door of the Bureau also?" Congreve asked.

"No, no. I have not the key. Only M. le Vicomte carries that, to my knowledge. Naturally he would lock his own Bureau before leaving for Bordeaux. It is there he keeps everything of value. Only the wines are in my charge. But at the hour this accident occurred, I was not in the *chai*."

"You can prove that?" was Congreve's query. "Where were you?"

"As to that, I shall say nothing until my master returns. I do not consider that you have the necessary authority. This is a matter for my employer and for the police."

"You prefer the police to me?" Congreve asked.

"Certainly," Jules replied.

"As you will," Congreve assented, with a sigh. "But you may have an opinion as to who might have ill wishes regarding this unfortunate woman, Madame Fürst."

"There are many, probably, who hated that one," Jules declared intolerantly. "No doubt she got what was due her."

"But surely," Congreve countered, "with all her faults, she was an amiable creature."

"Yes. Amiable first to one man, then to another. Amiable enough. But occasionally, these amiable hussies have to do with lovers not so amiable. It is not always easy to break off a *liaison*, you are doubtless aware," the old Frenchman declared. "This is a crime of passion, you will find. She went seeking one man and found the other. That is my belief. What a woman!"

The Gascon launched into a violent tirade in his native *patois*. I do not understand the Bordelais dialect over well, but had he spoken like a Parisian, he went far too fast for me to follow.

When his breath failed, Lewin broke in.

"What a mouthful! What does the old man say? Do you understand him?"

"Oh, yes," Congreve answered. "I understand him."

"Well, let us have it," Lewin said. "It's beyond me. What did he say?"

"He says he didn't like Madame," Congreve explained, with a shrug.

But Jules was only well started. He raved on impetuously. And this time his displeasure was vented upon the Yanks, some of whom had stolen his wines during the War, and upon Marty, whom he regarded as his accuser, and whom he in turn accused. Congreve sat back and let him scold till the old fellow had exhausted his ill humor. Then he took up the conversation once more.

"There are a few points still on which I would like to get your opinion, Jules," he explained, as calmly as though the Frenchman's little scene had never been. "Do you, perhaps, know any one by the name of Daniel?"

The Gascon shook his head.

"Or any one by the name of Percy?"

Again Jules answered in the negative.

"You say this Englishman living in the Château is the Vicomte's nephew? Has he been here long?"

"No," the Gascon answered. "He is almost a stranger. His home is in England. His mother was the Vicomte's sister, who married an Englishman. They say he is dead. I believe he was a chemist there and manufactured medicines. I have not seen the Vicomte's nephew for many years until three days ago But no—once, for a time, he came here, three weeks back. No, he is not one of the household. He is not one of us. I do not know why he is here."

Congreve changed the subject.

"In the *chai*, the floor is of earth throughout, I believe, Jules?"

"Yes, Monsieur, throughout."

"And was there, perhaps, a leak in the roof large enough for the rain to make mud here and there? Was there a spot where the floor would be damp at any time?"

"Not at all, Monsieur," Jules assured him. "The floor was uniformly dry at all seasons. There was no leak—no moisture. Occasionally, perhaps, there might have been a little wine spilled during the vintage, but always the floor is dry in my *chai*."

"Ah, thanks," said Congreve. "That may be useful. And the keys? How many keys were there to the building?"

"Only two sets, to my knowledge, Monsieur," the Gascon answered. "My own and my master's."

"And how many doors?"

"Three—only three," the *maître* explained. "The large door opening on the courtyard by which you entered yesterday, the small door into the vineyard at the other end, and the door on the gallery leading into the Bureau. Those three doors only."

"And, of course, the hole in the ceiling through which Marty descended?"

"Ah, yes, that," the Gascon agreed sourly.

"Good," said Congreve. "You have helped me very considerably, Jules. Now, you understand, *no one* must enter the *chai* until your master returns."

"I understand perfectly, Monsieur. But how can it be prevented? If some one unknown has a key, he will enter when he wishes. I cannot guard four openings."

"Of course not. But the doors may be nailed up and sealed. Then no one can enter without our knowledge, if you take reasonable precautions. My friend, M. Merton, will help you attend to this, Jules."

The Gascon got to his feet. "Very well, M. Congreve. It shall be done." He turned to go.

Congreve called after him. "But first, Jules, the cellar book, if you please."

The Gascon nodded. The door closed behind him.

"Look here, Congreve," I began, "do you intend to leave poor Madame Fürst lying in that Bureau with the door nailed shut? It seems to me some one ought to sit up with the body."

Congreve nodded. "Of course; it would only be decent. No doubt, the *maître* can arrange to have one of the servants stationed there. All I want is to have the *chai* shut up. *Nothing* must be touched until the Vicomte comes back. You can arrange for all this, surely."

"I think so," I said. "But wasn't Jules hot against Marty?"

Lewin had sat fidgeting, waiting for an opportunity to speak his mind. Now that it had come, he began without delay.

"That guy is a stubborn old cuss," he announced. "The nerve of him sitting there and accusing Marty of the crime. Marty never had anything against Madame. Marty knew I'd stand by him if he got caught in a jam. Suppose he *had* been caught stealing wine, I'd have looked out for him. Besides, I don't believe Marty could bring himself to strike a woman under any circumstances. But this old Frenchman is a hard nut to crack. Marty saw that blouse of his on *somebody*. Whoever it was must have known he had been seen, when he saw Marty's face in that hole. So he shed the blouse and beat it. Jules can't tell where he was, and it's plain to see he hated Madame Fürst. He and Arno are in cahoots on this deal, you can bet on it."

Congreve raised his hand to caution Lewin. "I hear Jules coming back," he said.

Lewin said no more. The door opened and Jules came forward to the table, carrying a great thick book like an overgrown ledger, which he laid before Congreve.

"*Voilà*, Monsieur. The cellar book," he said. Congreve got to his feet. I rose also, but Lewin remained seated, ignoring the Gascon.

"That is all now, Monsieur, that you wish of me?" Jules demanded.

"Only one thing more," Congreve said. "You have not touched your wine. Drink to the success of my investigation."

The Frenchman stood motionless for a moment, then reached forward and raised his glass high.

"Messieurs," he declared doggedly. "I drink to your frustration."

CHAPTER IV
THE EVIDENCE OF THE CELLAR BOOK

WHEN I RETURNED, I found Lewin pacing the floor of the *salon*, biting his nails in silent fury. He paused when he saw me.

"Oh it's you," he said. "Now we can march up and down together here."

"Why, what's the matter now?" I demanded. Lewin stopped and thrust his hands viciously into his pockets.

"Congreve's driving me crazy," he said. "Why I ever asked him to undertake this business is more than I can tell. He gives me a pain in the neck with all his trifling."

"What now?" I said wearily.

"Go into the dining room, and you'll see. *If* he'll let you stay there. He ran me out."

"What's he doing?"

"Nothing. Absolutely nothing. That is, nothing useful. For the last half-hour he's been sitting there lost to the world, poring over that damned cellar book, like a miser with his gold, utterly unaware that I was in the room. He's forgotten all about us and our troubles. Can't the man think of anything but drink?"

"Has it occurred to you, Mr. Lewin," I asked, "that, so far, practically everything that has been done in this case has been Congreve's doing?"

"Well," he countered, "that's what I'm kicking about. Nothing's been done. I'm going in there and give him a piece of my mind."

He strode towards the door of the *salle à manger*. I followed close at his heels. From the door, I saw Congreve. The cellar book

84

lay open on the table before him. On a small table alongside, he had ranged a dozen bottles of various shapes and sizes and all degrees of moldiness—some upright on their bottoms, others cradled in baskets. As the door clicked shut behind me, he looked up, his face aglow with satisfaction.

"Ah, Merton," he said, "you have lost no time. I have been busy too. And everything is ready. Now for the investigation. Behold, my suspects."

He waved towards the bottles on the smaller table.

"Your suspects?" I echoed stupidly.

"Yes. Certainly. You don't suppose I intend to sit here and guzzle wine myself without offering some to those who gratify me with their confidences? Surely you can't think so ill of me as that?"

"Damn it, Congreve," Lewin broke in. "This is not a wine supper."

"I only wish it were," said Congreve wearily. "Then you and I might get along better. For a man who claims that his first interest in life is fine wine, you seem surprisingly indifferent to it. If you learn no more at the other vineyards to which I conduct you than you have here, I am afraid you will have wasted my salary."

"I am afraid—" Lewin began, and I knew he was about to say that he had wasted it already. I therefore interrupted, to prevent any hard words.

"Explain yourself, Congreve," I demanded.

Congreve looked startled.

"Is any further explanation necessary?" he queried. "I should think it is perfectly plain. But I can put the whole secret in a nutshell! *In vino veritas*—by their wines ye shall know them. Drink with a man and you really get at him."

"Nonsense," said Lewin. "If you give a liar a drink, he'll only lie the more."

A shade of irritation crept into Congreve's voice. "Why do you drink at all, Lewin? I wonder."

Lewin mouthed his formula once more. "I drink because I feel good and want to feel better."

"Then drink, in heaven's name," said Congreve. "And I hope you'll soon feel better—much, much better. Frankly, your objections to my plans are becoming tiresome. Do you want me to go ahead with this investigation or have you a motive for blocking it? Are you trying to hinder justice?"

Lewin's face grew purple. He was on the point of another outburst. Once more I essayed the role of peacemaker.

"Come now, gentlemen," I said. "Let's not have trouble. There's enough to do. Go ahead, Congreve. Tell us what you are up to without any hocus-pocus, and let's get on with it."

"As you say," Congreve answered. "It's perfectly elementary. You are all well aware that a given bottle will produce quite different effects on different people, depending on their temperament and metabolism. Some men become sentimental, some silly, surly or mean, others destructive, genial, gay, clever, loquacious, silent, tender, amorous or despondent. The real character comes out, and the truth with it. Now if this murder was committed by some member of our dinner party, it should be possible to select some vintage which will induce in each one the desired reaction. Well, by this time, I suppose, you have all formed a conception of the inner character of each of our fellow guests. Certainly I have. I have accordingly tried to choose a bottle which, if my memory is not at fault, may help to bring them into the open and clear up our mystery. If none of these bottles has 'gone off,' something should result from my little experiment."

"So your idea is," Lewin broke in, "to get them all drunk and record what they tell you as evidence. A pretty mess you'll make of it."

"Not drunk, Lewin, not drunk. Surely you realize by this time that drunkenness disgusts me. But there is no doubt that a glass or two from the right bottle releases the essential spirit of a man. The liar lies more fluently—and so with the rest. A man's behavior when drunk may belie his real character, but a mere glass or two will reveal it. That, at any rate, is my conviction, my experience. It is all I have to go on."

"Well then, let's go," said Lewin. "Who is your first suspect?"

"I think," said Congreve, "we may as well call in the Englishman first. After all, you remember, we agreed we should consult him about our plan before we go ahead. I wonder where he is now?"

"He's out there in the reception room talking to Marty, I think," said Lewin. "At any rate, I heard him there a while ago."

"Then we can begin at once," said Congreve. "Would you mind asking him to come in now, Lewin?"

Without a word, Lewin turned to the door. As he opened it, he almost collided with Marty. The two men stood facing each other, neither, at first, willing to give way. Then Lewin brushed past his bodyguard.

Marty came on into the dining room. He was grinning in a self-satisfied way—in one hand the small decanter, in the other his glass. He came unsteadily, apparently sure of a welcome.

"Hello, Mr. Congreve," he said affably, and held up the decanter. "This is great stuff you gave me. By the way, I got somethin' else to tell you I clean forgot the first time."

"Good for you, Marty," Congreve answered. "What is it?"

"Well, Mr. Congreve, you know that barrel that I was rolling Madame over. It was in the aisle, wasn't it? Ain't that right?"

"Quite right, Marty. What about it?" Congreve asked.

"Well, I just remembered," Marty said, rocking on his heels. "That there barrel was already in the aisle when I come down the rope. I broke my shins over it the first thing. Somehow, when you come to think of it, that's funny, ain't it? I thought you'd like to know."

"Good for you, Marty. That may be important," Congreve agreed.

"You bet," said Marty gravely, and filling his glass unsteadily, turned slowly around and walked out through the doorway.

"Well, Merton," Congreve questioned me, "what have you to report?"

"Every one of the servants has an alibi from dinner on until just now. They were all gathered in the servants' hall enjoying the holiday feast provided by their master. Only the *maître de chai* was absent. He says he had started to the village to see a friend, but when the cold wind arose, being without his blouse, he turned back again."

"Hmn," said Congreve. "He was all alone, was he?"

"He says so," I agreed, "but he is a very surly fellow. Do you suppose he thinks his master had a hand in this murder and is preparing to take the blame for him?"

"It's not impossible," Congreve said. "Did you learn anything else? I see in your eye that you did."

"Yes," I said, "one little fact. One of the maids let it out that Madame Fürst was in the habit of addressing the Vicomte as Danielle. I'm afraid the poor girl will lose her job if the *maître de chai* has his way."

The door opened, and we heard the voices of Monkhouse and Lewin in animated conversation. A moment later, they came in.

Lewin began to question Monkhouse.

CHAPTER V
THE EVIDENCE OF THE ENGLISHMAN

"PERHAPS I HAD BETTER do the talking, Lewin," Congreve suggested, with a touch of asperity in his voice.

"All right," Lewin agreed. "I suppose there's no objection to my offering a suggestion from time to time?"

"None whatever," Congreve replied. "However, you asked me to take charge, and unless our investigation proceeds with some order, I am afraid it will come to nothing."

Turning to the Englishman, he added, "You see, Monkhouse, this is a ticklish business. In the absence of your uncle, it seemed that we should not sit idle, but try to do something to clear up this matter. I believe I know the Vicomte well enough to feel sure he would prefer to be consulted before the police are called in."

"We're not trying to butt in, you understand, Mr. Monkhouse," Lewin explained, breaking in again. "But you know how much red tape there is about the French law. I don't want the police—"

Monkhouse nodded.

"I understand, I think," was his comment. "Your man is rather involved, what?"

"Don't you go insinuating anything about Butch," Lewin began.

"Lewin, please," Congreve urged. "Don't lose your temper. There's no denying that Marty is a suspect—like all the rest of you. The point is, Monkhouse, I have agreed to conduct an investigation until your uncle returns from Bordeaux. You understand that I have no rating whatever as a detective. I fell in with Lewin's suggestion not because he made it, though he is my employer, but because I feel sure your uncle would approve. I think that he is entitled to have all the information we can gather laid before him as soon as he returns. If we neglect to take these precautions, many valuable clues may be overlooked or destroyed. I, personally, do not feel that I could undertake to call in the police—yet."

The Englishman remained puffing his pipe judicially, watching Congreve's plump face and deliberate motions.

"I am afraid it's quite irregular," he muttered superciliously.

"No doubt," Congreve agreed, with a smile. "Very irregular. And I assure you I shall not move in the matter without your consent. If you care to call in the police or to undertake the investigation in person, I am ready to withdraw. After all, you are the next of kin."

The Englishman shook his head decisively. "Aoh, damn it all. Not me, you know. Detecting is not my line, really. After all, I'm almost as much a stranger here as any of you. I fancy you know the Vicomte far better than I do. As a matter of fact, if you feel sure that he would approve, go ahead by all means. We don't want the village constable messing about here making every one uncomfortable. If you can find out anything, there's no harm done. I'd much prefer you took the responsibility. After all, my uncle is rather a peppery old boy. I suppose you haven't thought of sending after him?"

"Yes," said Congreve. "That is just what I wish to consult you about, among other things. I thought perhaps you might have a suggestion. Where can we find him?"

"That shouldn't be difficult," said Monkhouse, puffing away at his pipe.

"Splendid," said Congreve. "I was wondering if you would undertake to run in to Bordeaux at once and bring him back?"

"Why, yes, I suppose I could," the Englishman hesitated. "Of course."

"You have a car, you know," Congreve prompted.

"Of course," Monkhouse replied. "But first, I should like to know just what you have learned about this business. What am I to tell him when I find him? I must have something to tell him, you know." I detested his sneering tone.

"Fair enough," said Congreve. "Let's sit down, and I'll run over the details as nearly as I recall them."

We all acted on his suggestion, and he made a rapid resumé of Marty's story. Monkhouse listened attentively and without a single interruption. When Congreve had finished, the Englishman's pipe had gone out.

"Ghastly mess," was his comment. "Well, I suppose I must be off. Rather decent of you to send me after the old boy."

"I thought you'd want to be doing something," said Congreve. "It puts a better face on the matter to send for the Vicomte at once."

"Aoh, quite," said Monkhouse. "I sha'n't waste any time, I promise you."

He got to his feet.

"Before you go, however," said Congreve. "I should like to ask a few questions and learn what you know about this terrible affair."

The Englishman had charged his pipe and was lighting it again, sucking the flame into the bowl of his briar. When he had finished, he glanced up at Congreve.

"That won't take long," he answered. "Nothing! I know nothing whatever about it. The whole thing is a frightful shock to me, I assure you."

"I am afraid," said Congreve, "that won't do. I must ask every one in the Château to give some account of himself and his movements."

"I mean to say," said Monkhouse, "aren't you wasting time? There's no earthly good quizzing me. I tell you I know *nothing* about it."

"You may know more than you think," said Congreve, smiling with bland insistence. "You know, I suppose, where you were during the evening? You know something about the other persons here to-night? The questions I ask may seem futile and even impertinent, but the information gained may be of more value than you suspect. A few minutes, more or less, won't matter now. If you don't mind, please answer my questions. It will take only a short time. Then you can be on your way."

Monkhouse's pipe was going again; he sat down and relaxed in his chair.

"Go ahead," he said. "I'll do the best I can."

"Good," said Congreve. "When you left the dinner table, where did you go?"

"That's simple. I suppose you know what I was after. I knew my uncle wouldn't want a drunken lout prowling about the place and perhaps breaking into his cellar. That was why I volunteered to find something he might like to drink. So I went first to the cellar. When I got there, the door was locked, as I expected, and the servants were all in doors. The *maître de chai*, you may have noticed, is a crusty old beggar. He seems to have taken a dislike to me on account of the little affair in the *chai* this afternoon. I can't speak his *patois*, and I thought it very doubtful that he would help, even if I could let him know what I was after. So I thought I should unlock the cellar and help myself without troubling him. But when I went to do it, I found I hadn't my keys. You see, in changing for dinner, I had left them in a pocket of my tweeds."

"So you have keys to the wine cellar?"

"Aoh, yes. That is to say, I had."

"And where did you get these keys, may I ask?"

"Aoh, my uncle gave them to me," the Englishman explained, as though that were the most obvious thing in the world.

"Is that usual with the Vicomte? I should not have expected that."

"Nor should I," Monkhouse agreed. "The fact is, the old boy is not frightfully fond of me. He doesn't like to be pestered. I fancy he gave me the keys so as not to see more of me than necessary. We don't get along, you know. Well, I went over to my rooms to get the keys and help myself, as I told you. I saw no one in the courtyard. But as I went up the stairs, I was surprised. There was a light in my sitter. I couldn't remember leaving it on. I thought some one might be there, and when I went in, sure enough, I found some one in my rooms."

"Who was it?"

"Well, I don't like to speak ill of the dead, but the fact is, I found Madame Fürst there."

"Ah, Madame Fürst?"

"Yes. There she was."

"And what was she doing?"

"Well," said the Englishman, in obvious embarrassment, "the fact is, she was going through my things rather thoroughly, if you must know. Madame was a lady whose good qualities did not include that of fidelity. She was a very charming woman in her way, but frightfully mercenary. Any one who knew her will tell you so. The fact is, I had cut down her allowance to practically nothing, and I gathered she was taking this means of replenishing her purse. I was just in time to find her pocketing my spare change.

"Well, naturally, that annoyed me, you know. Of course, I was frightfully fond of her. You see, we've been friends for almost a year now. But after all, I mean to say, when you catch some one going through your clothes like that! I was annoyed, really."

"Go on," said Congreve. "This grows interesting."

"Yes. Isn't it? Well, to make a long story short, I made her disgorge."

"You mean you laid hands on her?"

"Aoh, no, nothing like that. But she knew that when I said 'no,' no it was. I sent her packing. She was only there a few minutes. She scuttled down the stairs, and that's the last I saw of her."

"What did you do then?"

"Well, of course, then I remembered what I had come for, and began fishing in my pockets for my keys. I couldn't find them. Then it occurred to me that very likely she had got away with them. I should have searched her, of course, but it was too late then. She was nowhere about.

"The cellar was locked. The keys were missing.

"Then I remembered that Lewin's man must be getting impatient, so I decided to take him something from my own private stock. Of course, I keep a few bottles in my sideboard. So I selected two and went back to the dining room, only to find everybody gone."

Congreve nodded.

"I noticed," he said, "that the bottles you brought were not at cellar temperature."

The Englishman's eyes twinkled. "You are rather good at sleuthing, after all, Congreve. I congratulate you."

Congreve raised a deprecatory hand.

"One gets to notice such things automatically," he said. "Did any one see you about the Château?"

"Can't say," said the Englishman. "I saw nobody."

"And you don't know where Madame Fürst may have gone after she left you?"

"I should think it's rather obvious where she went," said Monkhouse. "You say you found her key in the office door?"

Congreve fished the key ring from his pocket. "Are these the ones?"

The Englishman nodded briskly.

"Yes," he said. "The Vicomte's key ring. Perhaps you may know it."

"Now, Monkhouse," said Congreve, "only a few more questions. How long have you been here?"

"Aoh, for about a week, I should say."

"You've been here before, I suppose?"

"Occasionally. Three or four times. You understand, my mother was the Vicomte's sister. She married an Englishman, my father. I was reared in England. Once or twice as a boy I came here for short stays with my mother. After her death, I had no reason to come until lately."

"And what was that?"

"Well, you see, the Vicomte is rather a *bon vivant*, no business head. He was always in difficulties, and my father advanced considerable sums to keep him going. Then my father died, and when the depression came along, I rather thought my uncle might settle with the estate."

"You were hard up?"

"Well, I suppose that's a matter of opinion," said Monkhouse, smiling. "I never was stony broke, if that's what you mean. But after all, the factory wasn't doing so well. One must think of one's future, you know."

"You speak of a factory. What factory?"

"My father's—mine now," said Monkhouse. "We manufacture chemicals, if you must know."

"And your uncle paid his debt?"

"No. He couldn't do it, he said. The Château was mortgaged already, and of course, the vintage is bought up long before the grapes are harvested."

Congreve nodded.

"Well, he had no assets other than his cellar. Naturally, he didn't wish to part with that. So I proposed to find a buyer for the vineyard. He cut up a bit about that. But after all, what could he do? With things the way they are, nobody can tell what may happen. With all these Communists and Fascists about, and Cabinets going to pot every day, there might be a revolution any time, and we might lose everything. My idea was to cash in and take the money. I grant you, it may seem hard. But after all, this vineyard has changed hands many times and is none the worse for it. It was my money; I rather thought I should have it. So I found a buyer and brought him down to put it through."

"Mr. Everett Arno?" Congreve inquired.

"That's the chap," said the Englishman. "An American wine-grower. Plenty of money. Offered a good price. The thing was to be settled tomorrow. Now, I suppose, since this affair has come up, they will try to put me off for a bit. The French love a funeral, you know. The way they behave, one might think it was a Bank Holiday."

The Englishman's flippant tone jarred on me. But Congreve gave no sign. Then I remembered that the De Manny family was of English origin, dating back to the time of the Black Prince. A number of the old Bordeaux families are English. I suppose Monkhouse never once thought of his mother as a Frenchwoman.

"You're the heir to the vineyard then?" Congreve demanded.

"Rather not," Monkhouse replied, with a short laugh. "The Vicomte's son is in Algiers. Model young man, they say. Never met him. All I inherit from the Vicomte will be a bad taste in the mouth."

"He doesn't like you, then?"

"Why should he? Last time I was down here, I brought Madame Fürst along. My uncle had the bad taste to give her a glad eye. Well, I soon put a stop to that. The minute she knew he was stony broke, she gave him the cold shoulder, naturally. After that, of course, the old gentleman rather had it in for me."

"Do you happen to know any one by the name of Daniel? I mean any one here."

"Not a soul," said the Englishman. "That baffles me, I assure you."

"Ah," said Congreve. "Perhaps you know some one named Percy?"

"No, I assure you," said the Englishman. "That's beyond me." To Lewin, he added, "Your man's whole story seems frightfully improbable, if you know what I mean."

"Did you ever suspect," Congreve demanded, "that Mr. Everett Arno is not what he appears to be? Sailing under false colors?"

"Absurd," said the Englishman. "Why do you ask that?"

Congreve explained that Arno had been a bootlegger. "Marty said so."

"I can't believe it," said Monkhouse. "Ridiculous."

"This German, Fugger Bey," Congreve went on, "Can you tell us anything of him?"

"There's nothing to tell," said Monkhouse. "The Bey is interested in the chemistry of viticulture. The Germans, you know, have done wonders in that way—doctoring the soil of their vineyards—and their wine too, for that matter. I believe Arno had a notion the Bey might be useful to him here."

"You don't think the Bey might have murdered Madame Fürst?"

The Englishman looked startled. Then he considered.

"Never gave it a thought," he said. "He was much too fond of her for that, I should think—cautious fellow too. After all, why should he?"

"That's what I'm trying to find out," said Congreve dryly. "Just what do you know of Fugger Bey?"

"Next to nothing," said Monkhouse. "Aoh, yes. I do know something too. He is a Prussian, you know. Was an officer or something in the war in Turkey. That's where he picked up his title—training Turkish soldiers or something."

Congreve asked, "Is the Bey well off, do you know?"

"I'm sure I can't say. I rather fancy not. Immediately after the War, I understand he made rather a pretty penny selling German war materials secretly to some of the Balkan States. Got his name on the black list of the Allies doing that, of course. Daren't set foot in England, so he says."

Congreve smiled. "The Bey seems to have been on confidential terms with you."

"Aoh, no. It's no secret. He doesn't mind mentioning it. No doubt he thought he was justified. Of course, his activities were not considered quite nice by the Allies, but after all, I fancy plenty of Germans thought it patriotic. They haven't much use for the Treaty of Versailles, you know."

"Is the Bey a Nazi?" Congreve asked.

"I'm sure I don't know," said Monkhouse. "Might be if he found it worth his while. I never took any interest in Continental politics. Nasty business, if you ask me."

"Madame Fürst was rather expensive, I take it?" Congreve suggested.

"Ra-*ther*," said the Englishman fervently. "Restless too. Always looking for greener pastures. In the last six months, she's been going on with half a dozen chaps. I told you about the Vicomte. Well, when she found Arno was a rich man, she made up to him. Lately the Bey has enjoyed her favors. The fact is, she couldn't stick to any one long. Not that sort. But she always came back to *me*," Monkhouse explained complacently.

"And you didn't mind her defections?" Lewin asked curiously.

"Well, after all," Monkhouse defended his stand, "she had to think of herself first. One can't take a *liaison* too seriously. At any rate, I don't. Pleasure isn't everything. . . . Anything else?"

"I think that's all we need go into until you get back from Bordeaux."

"Righto," Monkhouse said. "I'll be off after the Vicomte. At this time of night, there'll be no traffic. I sha'n't be gone long, if I can find him. I suppose you're keeping the *chai* shut up?"

Congreve nodded.

"Cheerio."

A moment later, the Englishman was gone.

"Well," said Congreve, "he told us quite a lot."

"A lot of hooey," said Lewin. "You shouldn't have sent him. You'll never see the man again."

CHAPTER VI
THE EVIDENCE OF MRS. LEWIN

"WELL, MR. CONGREVE," said Lewin, "what are you going to do now?"

"I should like to have a word with your wife, Lewin, if you think she would grant us an interview at this late hour."

Lewin stared and was silent for a long minute. Then he nodded.

"I think I can arrange it. It isn't likely she'd be asleep, after what I told her."

"You have informed the ladies of the tragedy?" I asked.

"Yes. I ran up for a minute while you were with Jules," Lewin explained. "Congreve ran me out, you remember. I had to talk to somebody. I'll run up and bring her down for you."

"I think we had better receive her in the *salon*," said Congreve considerately.

"Good idea," Lewin agreed.

In a surprisingly short time, Mrs. Lewin came down, fully dressed, and joined us in the *salon*.

"Now, Mrs. Lewin," Congreve said, "I would like to ask if you can tell me anything about this terrible affair. Your husband and I have agreed that we should investigate the whole matter at once, and we cannot afford to overlook anything which might help."

Mrs. Lewin stood very erect under the chandelier in the *salon*, and the light from above made her worn face look even more haggard than it had seemed in the sunlight. For all her expensive clothes, she had a hard, gaunt look—as of some pioneer woman. She fumbled a little with her beads as she stood regarding us. It was evident that the murder had shaken her, and also, perhaps, stiffened her. There was something uncompromising about her, something unrelenting. She seemed strangely out of place among the Louis Quinze chairs, the tapestries and marbles, the gilt and mirrors of that aristocratic old room.

"Is this true, Richard?" she demanded.

"Yes, Mamma," said Lewin. "We must all help. If this can be cleared up at once, we shall be saved a peck of trouble. In France they say one is considered guilty until he is proven innocent. We want to solve it before it comes into the hands of the police, if possible. I don't want my trip interfered with."

"So that's it," she said coldly. "Very well. I don't think I can be of any use, Mr. Congreve."

"All I ask," said Congreve, "is that you tell us just what your movements were since we came to the Château this afternoon, and also answer a few questions."

"I don't think I can be of the least use," she repeated. "Miss Simpson and I were together when Richard brought the news and we have remained together ever since. I know nothing about it, except what Richard told me."

"Miss Simpson was with you all the time?"

"Yes, poor thing. And now she's almost hysterical. I'm afraid Richard didn't break the news very gently. She can't stand such excitement."

"Then it appears that both of you ladies have an alibi," said Congreve.

"Yes," said Mrs. Lewin. "We have."

"Well, then, I sha'n't be long," Congreve said, evidently trying to put her at her ease. "Suppose you go ahead and tell me just what you have been doing since you came to the Château."

"Well," said Mrs. Lewin. "I don't think I know anything worth telling—nothing that you are not aware of already. We drove up together, you remember, late in the afternoon, and got out at the front door. I waited with Richard while you went to meet the master of the house. When you came back with him and the others, you remember that I refused the Vicomte's invitation to taste his wines.

"Yes," said Congreve, "I remember."

"I don't approve of liquor in the first place," she said. "If Richard had taken my advice, he wouldn't be in this fix. No good ever came of alcohol, but there's no use talking to Richard."

"Now, Mamma," said Lewin soothingly, "let's not go into that here."

Mrs. Lewin proceeded as though she had not heard her husband.

"Once," she said, "Richard took me with him to taste wine. Once was enough. It's disgusting, I think. All that spitting—and indoors too—though I suppose it's less dangerous than swallowing the stuff would be. Well, you all went into the *chai*, and I told Miss Simpson we had better go for a walk in the garden of the Château."

"And what did Miss Simpson say?"

Mrs. Lewin looked surprised at the question. Her voice betrayed no sense of humor.

"Miss Simpson always says 'yes' to me," she explained.

"So you went into the garden?"

"Yes. We walked in the garden for perhaps twenty minutes. Then we came back and waited in the front yard for you. I don't like French gardens—all gravel and evergreens and marble—too much like a cemetery. We waited where you found us when you came out."

"Ah, yes," said Congreve. "And after that?"

"Well, after that, Richard told us that he was going into the cellar with his host, and I waited with Miss Simpson until he came out. Then he informed us that we were to spend the night here and that our bags had been carried in. We went up to dress for dinner."

"Ah, yes," said Congreve. "And where are your rooms?"

"They are upstairs," Mrs. Lewin explained, "over the wine cellar. My room looks out on the courtyard. Miss Simpson's opens from mine, but is on the other side of the house, overlooking the kitchen garden.

"We were there until dinner time and came down together. We waited in the *salon* while the company gathered and went in to dinner with you, as you remember. We were at table until Richard began quarreling. Then I took Miss Simpson upstairs, and we had dinner. Now the poor thing's hysterical."

"Mrs. Lewin, have you ever seen any of these people before?"

"No," said Mrs. Lewin positively. "And what's more, I hope I never see any of them again. I don't understand these Continentals, and what's more, I don't like them. All their ideas seem foolish and wicked to me. I don't know why Richard brought me along over here. If he weren't my husband, I'd say it served him right for coming on such an errand. He's too old to be gallivanting around, following after strong drink."

"Then you have no suspicion who might have committed the crime?"

"Any of them might have committed it, for all I know," Mrs. Lewin said doggedly. "Killing people seems to come natural to Continentals. They are always at each other's throats. Their history ever since the beginning has been nothing but one murderous war after another. They fooled us once into fighting their battles and then fooled us again into paying for them. I should think that would be enough for any American, without coming over here to make friends with them. There isn't a decent person in the whole lot of them, in my opinion.

"What can you expect of a man who spends his life making and selling liquor, like the Vicomte? Or a rat like that Arno? Heaven knows how many men he's murdered. That Englishman is so stuck up he gives me a pain. And if there's anything in faces, that German fellow is an out-and-out crook."

"You mean Fugger Bey?" Congreve prompted.

"Yes, that Hun with the beard. He's too polite and smooth to be genuine. I don't trust him—always smiling and bowing, but his eyes are cold as ice. He's a vain man, Mr. Congreve, cruel and vain. That's what I think of him. If he didn't do it, it must be the Frenchman. It's hard to believe that an American, or even an Englishman, would strike a woman and throw her into a barrel of wine."

"You don't think Marty could be guilty then?"

"Butch Marty?" she exclaimed hotly. "No, not even when he was drunk. You'll make a big mistake if you try to pin anything on Marty, Mr. Congreve."

"But, my dear lady," said Congreve, "I'm not trying to pin anything on anybody. I'm trying to find out the truth. That's all."

"Then you'd better find out something about that hussy who was murdered. Where I live, they'd have run her out of town in no time. Why, she even made eyes at Richard. No doubt some man led her astray in the beginning. But it's my honest opinion that when she passed on, the world was well rid of her. Oh, I know you think I'm uncharitable. But after all, what harm has been done, really? Everybody's better off now she's gone. How charitable will *you* be, if you catch the man who killed her?"

"My dear Madame," said Congreve.

But Mrs. Lewin would not listen. "Please don't 'Madame' me, sir. I'm an American, thank God. Call me Mrs. Lewin, if you please. I don't want any foreign handles to my name. It makes me sick to think of our soldier boys coming over here to fight for a country which tolerates such creatures."

"Now, Mamma," said Lewin.

"Don't you take up for her, Richard," said Mrs. Lewin, and there was battle in her voice. "I've had all I can stand to-day. As for you, Mr. Congreve, I have told you all I know. You've lived here a long time, of course, but you should still have more sense than to believe any American would commit a crime like this."

"Almost any one might commit a murder, Mrs. Lewin, under sufficient provocation," said Congreve coolly. "Even women have been known to do such things—women who never touched a drop of liquor—women who never stepped from the path of virtue. But now I wonder if you would do me one more favor? I should like to have a few words with your friend, Miss Simpson."

Mrs. Lewin did not waver. "You can't see her now," she announced, with finality. "The poor thing is all used up. Later perhaps, when she's cooled down, but not now."

"Very well, Mrs. Lewin," said Congreve. "I'll postpone my interview with Miss Simpson until you have prepared her for it."

Congreve and I went back into the dining room. Lewin followed us to the door.

"You mustn't mind my wife," he said, in a subdued tone. "She's not like this ordinarily. The business has upset her. She's prejudiced, you know. For years, she was a pillar of a Temperance

Society. The collapse of Prohibition and everything has put her nerves on edge. I think I'd better stay with her for a little while. I'll join you in a few minutes."

He closed the door. Congreve and I looked at each other.

"Phew," I said. "What a harridan!"

"No, no," said Congreve. "Not a harridan, a fanatic. She's drunk ice water so long it has frozen her up. That woman has had some great shock in the past which has embittered her. Somehow or other, this business is connected in her mind with her trouble."

"But how?" I demanded. "How could it be? What's it to her? She has an alibi."

"Ah, that's the question," said Congreve. "Has she an alibi? And *if* she has, she may be shielding some one else. She's as fierce as a she-bear that has lost its cub. Accusing me of trying to pin this crime on Butch Marty! What is Butch Marty to her?"

"I don't know," I said. "She certainly is fond of the poor sot."

I told Congreve what I had witnessed between them in the courtyard that afternoon. He listened attentively.

"Can it be that she loves the mutt?" I said.

"Hardly that," Congreve agreed. "Lewin is evidently in the know. He understands her attitude, if we could get it out of him. Probably she's fearful for Marty. But it can hardly be love. She's too straight-laced a woman for that sort of an affair. And Lewin doesn't look to me the kind of man who would tolerate such an irregularity in his family. She hasn't a penny of her own; I happen to know that. The money is all Lewin's. And she's not so unworldly as you might suppose. She has a taste for luxury too, as she understands luxury. She's not going to do anything that would drive her husband away. No, there's something hidden here. Something that we don't know about."

Congreve suddenly smiled. "It all reminds me of a sign I saw once in a French hotel which was making an effort to cater to American tourists. It advertised ICE WATER AT DISCRETION. I'm afraid the dear lady has used more ice water than discretion in her diet."

"Well," I said, "if these are its effects, in future I shall guard against ice water."

"But if she loves her husband," Congreve went on, "maybe it's Lewin she's trying to protect."

"From the hussy or the wine?" I asked.

"From both, perhaps. You know, in these days nothing is easier than getting a divorce, unless it is falling off a horse. The fact is, it's much easier to get rid of a wife than to rid one's self of a mistress. Mrs. Lewin is terribly small-town, no doubt, but she is not so stupid as she seems. One must remember that she doesn't know the whole story Marty told us. All she knows is that Marty was found locked in with the dead woman's body. She's the kind to hate Madame Fürst's sort like poison, and especially if Madame made a pass at her own husband. She's in a constant state of alarm and anxiety lest poor old Lewin should drink too much and get into trouble. Moreover, she doesn't like people to disagree with her or oppose her in any way. You recall what she said of Miss Simpson?"

"That she always says 'yes'?" I queried.

"Precisely. She distrusts Frenchmen because she believes they are all abandoned to wine, women, and song. And she distrusts all men, even Americans, who like or have to do with alcohol."

"You, for instance?" I suggested.

"Me, particularly," Congreve nodded. "After all, I am the man who is guiding her husband along the downward path."

We both laughed outright.

"But you notice that the one she hates most venomously is the German, Fugger Bey. She called him a Hun."

"That was strange," I said. "It has been fifteen years since anybody referred to the Germans as Huns. What has she been thinking of all these years?"

"That," said Congreve, "is probably her secret. And there's something else about her, too. Didn't you notice?"

"No," I confessed. "I don't know what you mean."

"The scent she wore. It filled the *salon.*"

"True enough," I agreed. "It was strong."

"The same heavy scent that she wore at dinner, that her husband made such a fuss about. You remember?"

"Of course," I agreed, "but it seemed much stronger just now."

"That is my point," said Congreve. "She put more of it on just before she came down to talk to us."

"A perverse lady," was my comment.

"Perverse and stubborn," said Congreve. "Her mind automatically transforms the physiological effects of wine into sins."

"You don't suppose she could have murdered Madame Fürst?" The speculative light came into Congreve's eyes.

"And yet," he said, "was it perversity or was it precaution?"

"Precaution?" I echoed, mystified. "Precaution against what?"

"Well, no doubt," said Congreve, "you noted that wine stain on her husband's waistcoat? Don't you suppose she noticed that? She's a vigilant person."

"I confess, I hadn't noticed any wine stain," I explained.

"Not notice it!" Congreve exclaimed. "How could you miss it? It is possible that she believes Lewin murdered the woman and acquired the wine stain on his clothes in doing so. If our hypothesis is correct, she may be trying to shield him, as well as Marty. If she saw that stain, she may have feared that some one would smell it. After all, you know, she was present when I identified those bottles at dinner. She may have worn the scent to kill the odor of the wine."

"There was enough of it to kill anything, I should say."

"Very true," said Congreve, "but she was a little late. When Lewin came back to the dinner table, I knew by his furtive air that he had been up to something. I spotted the stain at once."

"Then they might both be in it? That would make it premeditated—a conspiracy."

"Yes," said Congreve slowly and doubtfully. "It's not utterly impossible. But Lewin didn't get that wine stain in the *chai*—at any rate, not from a cask. I suspected he had been up to something—opening a bottle on the sly—and planned to twit him with it. You may have noticed that I dropped my serviette at his feet as we stood in the dining room?"

"So you did."

"Well, that gave me an opportunity to bring my nose close to his waistcoat as I stooped to pick it up. The wine on his waistcoat was not from the casks of Château Roet, Merton. Young wine has a fruity fragrance quite unlike that of a bottled vintage. The wine on Lewin's waistcoat came out of an old bottle, Merton. I imagine it must have been a bottle of sweet Sauterne."

CHAPTER VII
THE EVIDENCE OF MR. ARNO

"I THINK WE HAD better consult Arno next," Congreve said, getting to his feet, "if we can still find him at the hotel in the village. Let's put on our coats and trot down there. A turn in the fresh air will do us both good."

Within fifteen minutes, the two of us had reached the hotel, and after a word with its portly proprietor, we made our way up the stairs and along the corridor to a door on which was the number "7." Congreve knocked.

The door opened a crack, and Arno's dark, suspicious face was partly visible. It was very evident that we were not welcome.

Congreve answered the man's unspoken question.

"Mr. Arno, I have come here to have a little talk with you."

"Yeah," he answered, without budging. "Well, I'm busy."

Congreve ignored his rebuff and went on pleasantly, "A murder has been committed at the Château."

"Yeah, so I hear."

"That's what I want to talk about—with you," Congreve explained blandly.

The dark face never altered, and there was a pause before Arno replied. Indeed, all through our conversation with him that night, I observed a pause each time before he answered Congreve, as though he were thinking in one language and translating his words into the best English he knew before communicating his thought.

"I dunno nothin' about that," he said. "I left the Château before it happened."

"All the same," said Congreve, "I think it will be to your advantage to talk with me, Arno. I have no official authority and am in no way connected with the police. But, in the Vicomte's absence, I have decided to gather all the information possible so that it may be laid before him on his return from Bordeaux. It is necessary that I talk with you, as well as with all the others who were in the Château to-night."

"I got no time to talk, I tell you. If you ain't a detective, why not mind your own business? Beat it."

Arno tried to close the door.

Congreve had evidently foreseen this possibility. His foot was against the door and the weight of his plump body rested heavily upon it.

"Just one word more, Arno," he said. "There is reason to believe that an American named Rauh—Goosey Rauh, to be specific—has some connection with this crime. It happens that you resemble him very strikingly."

"So what?" said Arno, unrelenting.

"If the police are called in immediately, they will very likely arrest you on suspicion and hold you for questioning. The cells in the village jail are very uncomfortable, I understand. I think you will save time and probably inconvenience if you do as I wish."

"I got nothin' to say," Arno protested, scowling.

"Well, I have," said Congreve, raising his voice, "and I intend to say it. I came here to have a talk with you, and I'm going to have it—now. If you want to talk through the door so that everybody in the hotel can hear what is said, have it your own way. If you prefer a private chat, open the door and we'll come in."

For a minute there was silence.

Then Congreve went on. "If neither of these alternatives appeals to you, of course I can call in the gendarmes now. The proprietor of this hotel is the mayor of the town. His brother is what you would call the chief of police. He lives next door. The *Mairie* is just across the street. If you prefer to spend the night in the cells there, very well. If not, admit me."

"So the chief of police is a friend of yours?" Arno sneered.

"He's the friend of all honest men," said Congreve, unflinching. "Make up your mind—yes or no?"

"Okay," said Arno, and opened the door wide enough to admit us in single file.

I followed Congreve in. Our unwilling host closed the door behind us. I noticed his right hand remained in his coat pocket.

Congreve sat down and I followed his example.

On the bed lay an open bag, and alongside the contents of the chest of drawers. Arno had evidently been packing.

"Making an early start?" Congreve asked blandly.

"I got business in Bordeaux," said Arno sullenly.

"Lucky I caught you before you got away," said Congreve,

"All right," said Arno, "let's go. What's on your mind?"

"Do you know any one by the name of Percy?" Congreve demanded.

"No," said Arno. "I dunno Percy."

"Or Daniel?" Congreve demanded.

Again the pause preceded the dark man's reply. "Yeah," he said, nodding. "That's what this Madame Fürst called the Vicomte."

Congreve sat up, interested.

"You heard that yourself?" he demanded.

"Sure I heard it—three times."

"Go on," Congreve urged.

"That's all," said the dark-faced man. "She called him Daniel, or something that sounded like it. She talked kind of funny, you know. She's a Roumanian."

"You're from California, I understand?" Congreve questioned. "Interested in the wine business?"

"That's my business," Arno replied ambiguously.

"I've always wished I knew more of the California wines," Congreve proceeded blandly. "Over here, of course, one doesn't have much opportunity, but I hear some of them are excellent. What brands do you handle?"

"Say, what are you after, anyhow? I got no time to waste. I got nothin' to say. You don't fool me none. You've been listening to that pot-bellied millionaire's trigger man. He's trying to put me in the middle, but he'll never do it. If you want to believe a chiseler like that, go and talk to him. That bat caught him stealin' wine, and he blotted her out. You might say she asked for it. Anybody could see she's copper-hearted. But I got nothin' to do with it. And I got *nothin'* to say."

"What do you know about Monkhouse?" Congreve demanded, ignoring Arno's words.

"Plenty. He ribbed me into coming here. Everything he had was on the cuff up to then. Everything would be jake now, if it hadn't been for that damn dropper. If he don't lay off me, I'll put the cross on him."

The language of the underworld, into which Arno had dropped in his excitement, apparently baffled Congreve,

"I'm afraid I don't understand," he declared.

Immediately, Arno was conscious of his error. Abruptly he got up, and without a word, walked over and opened the door.

"Okay," he countered, recovering himself. "As the Frogs say, *feenee*," jerking his thumb at the door. "Outside, you guys," he ordered.

It was evident that no more could be got out of Arno. Congreve and I got to our feet and walked to the door.

"Don't forget, you're invited to lunch at the Château to-morrow, Arno," Congreve reminded him.

"I'll be back," Arno answered, "maybe."

"You'll not be back," said Congreve, "for you're not going anywhere. You'll stay."

"Everybody else walked out; why pick on me?"

"The party won't be complete without you," Congreve explained. "But since you don't like this hotel, I suggest that you come back with me to the Château. There's plenty of room there, and I may want to see you again later. The police aren't likely to interfere with us there, you see. I don't intend to call in the police until the Vicomte turns up. If you try to leave now, the police will certainly regard it as a suspicious circumstance. And if you remain in the hotel, your resemblance to Goosey Rauh might easily be noticed in the daylight. You'll be much better off at the Château. How about it?"

To my surprise, Arno assented.

"Okay," he said.

Going back into the room, he bent over the open suitcase on the bed. His body shielded it from our view, but he was apparently transferring something to the inside pocket of his coat. That done, he turned and came out into the hall and locked the door.

"Let's go," he said.

Downstairs, he stepped into the bar and bought a small bottle of cognac. While he was gone, I spoke to Congreve.

"I'm not sure I want to travel with our friend, Arno, at night and unarmed," I said.

"Nonsense," said Congreve. "If he's an honest man, we have nothing to fear. If he's the crook I think he is, he won't dare attack me."

We all got into the waiting taxi, and a few minutes later, the taxi stopped at the gates of the Château. Nothing had been said on the way up.

"*Attendez*," Arno commanded the driver.

And we all turned towards the gates. Before we could enter, another car came roaring up the road from the direction of Bordeaux and turned in towards the gate, throwing its strong light upon us.

"Ah," said Congreve, with relief, "the Vicomte's back again."

He stepped up to the car, took hold of the door handle, and opened it to greet his friend. But there was no response.

I heard Congreve question the chauffeur and Henri's volley of excited French in reply.

"Henri, where is M. le Vicomte?"

The chauffeur answered volubly, "Ah, Monsieur, who knows? I cannot say. He entered the car, as you remember, and I drove from the Château straight to Bordeaux. I drove fast, Monsieur. You know that M. le Vicomte was always in a hurry on the road. I stopped nowhere. I made good time, but when we arrived at the house of the notary in the Quai des Chartrones, and I got down and opened the door for my master, there was nobody in the car. Nobody, you comprehend. It was empty. There was only this."

The chauffeur leaped from his seat, and thrusting his head and shoulders into the car, produced his master's portfolio. Emerging again, he went on.

"Only these papers. The street was empty. He was nowhere about. He could not have slipped from the car without my seeing him. It was impossible. I did not know what to do. I was frightened. Then I thought perhaps he had fallen from the car or leaped out. But how could he have done that, I ask you, through the closed door? The window is small, you see, and if he had stood on the running board and closed the door, I must have heard it. What had happened, Monsieur? What was I to do?"

"Return, I suppose, and look for your master along the route," Congreve prompted.

"Yes, Monsieur," Henri agreed, grateful that Congreve approved his action, "that is what I did. And now I am here. Perhaps M. le Vicomte is here before me?"

"You are quite sure you did not stop on the way in?"

"Nowhere, Monsieur, nowhere."

"Nor slowed down, perhaps, a little?"

"Only on the bridge into the city," Henri reported, "only on the bridge. And very little then."

"Still, he might have eluded you there, perhaps?" Congreve prompted.

"No, Monsieur, I cannot believe it. It seems impossible. How could he and why should he? It is too much for me. I can only think that M. le Vicomte is here in the Château still."

A silent, burly figure came out of the shadows into the lights of the cars. It was the *maître de chai*. He seemed to know all that had passed and showed no surprise at his master's disappearance.

"The Vicomte," he assured Henri, "is not in the Château."

"What's all this about?" said Arno. "What are they saying? They talk too fast for me."

"The Vicomte is missing," I explained.

"The hell he is," said Arno angrily. "So that's why he wouldn't take me with him!"

The *maître de chai* addressed Congreve. "Monsieur, since we talked together, I have remembered something overlooked before. That name Danielle which Madame Fürst was heard to call out I remember now to whom it belongs, Monsieur. The maid, Marie, informed M. Merton that she had heard Madame apply it to my master, the Vicomte. The girl is mistaken. Madame used that name only for her friend, M. Monkhouse."

"You are sure of this, Jules?" Congreve questioned.

"Quite sure, Monsieur," Jules answered steadily.

"But that name is Italian," I protested.

"But naturally, Monsieur," Jules replied. "Madame Fürst spoke Italian very well."

Congreve was looking at the *maître de chai*. "You think the Vicomte's nephew is involved in this crime, Jules?"

Jules shrugged his shoulders and pursed up his lips. "Who knows, Monsieur? But I ask then, where is he?"

CHAPTER VIII
THE EVIDENCE OF THE BUTLER

AT THE CHÂTEAU, Congreve saw that Arno was safely installed in a room at the top of the stairs and stationed a servant to watch his door.

"Now," he said, "I suppose Miss Simpson may have calmed down sufficiently to give us an audience. At any rate, I intend to try. Bring that bottle of Chablis along, Merton. It's a gay wine and can do no violence to the poor girl's rather fragile brain."

I followed him up the stairs, and after a brief conference with the Lewins, we were admitted to a great chamber where Miss Juliette Simpson was lying in a mahogany four-poster, heavily curtained with lace.

The interview was brief, but much too long for my taste. In fact, the interview with Miss Simpson was almost entirely fruitless. She had been hysterical and was, when we saw her, restored to her normal state of vacuous silliness. A more vacant, inconsequent, and brainless young woman has never come to my notice, and I hope sincerely never may.

All Congreve's efforts to direct the conversation or to elicit any intelligent response to his questions were wasted. The only fact we got out of her was entirely irrelevant to the matters discussed. But she laughed so much over it that Congreve had to let her tell him that Mrs. Lewin's husband had once been a manufacturer of barrels. His barrels had been used for whisky, apparently, and Mrs. Lewin was ashamed of the fact, and threw it up to Lewin as often as they had an argument. This stupid fact of family history seemed to be the brightest gem of humor known to Miss Simpson, and she giggled over it until Congreve and I politely took our leave.

"How do people like that survive?" I demanded, as we went down the stairs together. "They're so dumb it doesn't seem possible."

"You're right," he assented fervently. "It's one of the wonders of nature. The fellow who invented the theory of the survival of the fittest should have met Miss Simpson and saved himself the trouble. Do you know what she reminds me of?"

"I should be charmed to hear."

"Of the three monkeys. You remember. That little group which used to be in every gift shop. *She hears no evil; she sees no evil; and she speaks no evil.* I'm afraid, Merton, that as a detective, I am a splendid beginner. Only an amateur would have thought it worth his while to question Miss Simpson."

"Never mind," I encouraged him. "Let's try the butler. There's nothing like an old family servant. Robert ought to be a perfect mine of information about this household and its guests."

"No doubt," said Congreve, without enthusiasm, "but I am beginning to doubt my fitness for the role of miner."

For all that, Congreve summoned Robert.

The butler appeared promptly, very English and correct, though obviously sleepless. He explained that he had come from England two years before on the death of his former master, Monkhouse senior. He had done this at the request of young Mr. Monkhouse, who had been forced to sell the family home and had taken rooms in town. As to a theory of the crime, he preferred not to express himself, but it was evident to me that he thought the Vicomte guilty.

"Can you tell us anything of Madame Fürst?" Congreve asked him.

"Oh, yes, sir; I think I can, sir. I got to know her rather well, sir. She was a Roumanian, or perhaps I should say a Hungarian. She was from Transylvania. She was a bit of a linguist."

"Ah," said Congreve, "and how did you get to know her so well?"

"Oh, sir, she was often here. The fact is, sir, she was the mistress of M. le Vicomte until Mr. Monkhouse arrived, sir. I'm afraid Madame Fürst was a mercenary person, sir. The Vicomte had no money, of course. Mr. Monkhouse had, or seemed to have. He stole her from under the Vicomte's nose."

"Let's see," Congreve prompted, "Mr. Monkhouse's name is Percy, isn't it?"

"Bertie, sir. Bertrand it should be, but they call him Bertie."

"Oh, yes, I remember," Congreve assented. "I heard Madame Fürst call him that yesterday afternoon. You don't happen to know any one by the name of Percy here?"

"Percy? I think not, sir."

"Or Persée?" Congreve questioned. "That's the French for Perseus, you know."

"No, sir, I can't recall having ever heard that name, sir."

"Did you know any one named Daniel? It seems Madame Fürst called aloud for Daniel shortly before she was murdered."

"Did she, sir? Daniel, did you say, sir? But it must have been Danilo, sir. That's the name she always used for her lover of the moment, sir. She called each of them that in turn—M. le Vicomte, Mr. Monkhouse, Mr. Arno—all of them in turn."

"What makes you think Monkhouse made a pass at her? Did he really care about the woman?"

"I'm sure I can't say as to that, sir. He may have done it just to annoy his uncle. You see, M. le Vicomte had to put up with a good deal from his nephew. Mr. Monkhouse was rather hard up at times. A great spendthrift, you know. As the French say, a leaking cask. Money burned his pockets."

"Do you know what business brought him here? I suppose it wasn't family affection?"

"Oh, no, sir," the butler assured him, "not that, I think, sir. The fact is, Mr. Monkhouse came to arrange for the sale of the Château. He brought a buyer, a Mr. Arno, with him. I gathered he expected rather a handsome commission from the buyer when the sale was made. When M. le Vicomte found that out, he was in a rage, sir— something terrible."

"And do you think it possible Mr. Monkhouse had a hand in this crime?"

"Well, sir, I can't say, sir. But I should think you'll soon find out. If Mr. Monkhouse is in it, I don't think you need expect him back. He's soft, sir, if you'll pardon my saying so, sir. He's not the lad to come back and face the music, sir."

"Did Madame know of this deal with Mr. Arno?"

"Oh, yes, I think so, sir. She took great interest in money matters."

"Do you know whether the Vicomte gave a key to the cellar to his nephew?"

"I can't say, sir. Perhaps he did. Mr. Monkhouse is a very exacting young man. If he asked his uncle for a key, he got it, sir."

"What do you think of Mr. Arno? Have you any opinion?"

The butler stiffened. "I have, sir. He's no gentleman."

"And Fugger Bey? Has he been here before?"

"Yes, sir, with Mr. Arno, sir." Robert sniffed.

"I take it you don't like the Bey, either?"

"No, sir. The servants complain that he never tips, sir."

"Well, Robert, thanks for your information. I think that will be all for the present."

"Yes, sir. Thank you, sir."

Robert prepared to withdraw.

CHAPTER IX
THE EVIDENCE OF THE BEY

THERE WAS A KNOCK at the door. Robert looked at Congreve inquiringly. Congreve nodded, and the butler stepped to the door. A moment later, he was back.

"Fugger Bey to see you, sir."

Congreve smiled. "Good, let him in."

The butler opened the door, admitted the caller, and then withdrew.

Congreve rose and greeted his visitor.

"Come in," he said. "I am delighted to see you. I've been wanting to see you ever since dinner, but the proprietor of the hotel said you were out."

The Bey bowed gravely from the hips and took the chair Congreve had offered him.

"What is it," he asked, in his careful English, "you wish of me?"

"Just a few questions which may help us find the man guilty of this murder," Congreve explained. "But first, suppose we fortify ourselves with a glass of something? I suppose you have no objection to drinking French wine?"

Fugger Bey laughed. "Certainly not. In Germany we have a proverb—perhaps you know it. We say 'We don't like the Frenchman, but we like his wine.'"

I saw the speculative look in Congreve's eyes pass into one of certainty as he regarded the Bey's smiling, crafty face, and I knew that Congreve had selected the bottle already which he thought best suited to draw out the German.

"Good. Justice is the work of kings. To feel like a king, one must drink the wine of kings. I suggest a Burgundy. Suppose we try this Montrachet 1911. If this bottle is like the last I tasted of that vintage, it should prove satisfactory."

When the glasses had been lifted, the conversation went forward again.

The Bey explained himself. He was, he said, a Prussian, and had been an officer throughout the War. He had served in several branches, but at the last had found the work he liked best in chemical warfare. He told with considerable pride and some amusement of his success in outwitting the Allies and selling German war materials under their noses to several of the Balkan States. Finally that enterprise had come to an end. He boasted also of his exploits in smuggling drugs over the borders of various countries. It was his practice, he said, to get himself up like a tourist with a knapsack and stick, and carry the contraband over the border on foot. The hospitals in some of the countries could not afford to pay duty on the drugs they dispensed and were glad to connive with him. But of late years, this had become so dangerous that he had been compelled to give it up. Recently, he said, he had attached himself to Mr. Arno. Arno was interested in scientific winegrowing, in which the Germans excelled.

"Consider our host, the Vicomte," he sneered. "He only gets a good vintage once in three or four years. As a result, he goes bankrupt—simply because he is so stupid as to let nature take its course. We Germans know better than that. Chemical analysis has taught us many things of which the Frenchman knows nothing. The analysis of soils and of wines has enabled us to create good wines every season."

"Ah, yes," said Congreve. "But don't you think the real charm of wine lies in the fact that it is a living thing—a natural product? Isn't it a fact that the most thorough chemical analysis shows practically no difference as between a really great wine and a very poor wine of the same general type?"

The German's cold blue eyes no longer twinkled. "I thought," he said, "you wished to ask me questions concerning this crime."

"I do, I do," Congreve agreed. "In fact, I am."

"Well, then," said the Bey, "the point I wish to make is simply this. Arno has unusual business ability and plans to use my skill and knowledge in his business. He came here to buy Château Roet. We plan to expand the vineyard by scientific methods and to produce vastly greater quantities of this famous wine. There's surely nothing mysterious about that."

Congreve demanded, "Has Mr. Arno ever explained the nature of his business in the United States?"

"I only know that he was interested in selling wines there."

"You've never heard that Mr. Arno was a well-known bootlegger in the States?"

"What you call a crook?" the German asked, displaying his knowledge of American slang.

"Precisely," said Congreve.

"No, I never suspected that," said the Bey. "I can't believe that. But if it were true that he violated your Prohibition, it was only what every one approved, was it not? If the Americans tolerated him as a bootlegger, they can surely have no objections to his selling wine, now that it is legal."

Congreve's voice had a touch of asperity.

"It takes more than good soil and knowledge and skill to produce great wines," he said.

"Ah, yes," said the Bey. "You mean the chemistry."

"I mean character," said Congreve.

"You object to the chemistry?" the German protested.

"I object to murder," said Congreve.

"Ah, then," said the Bey insolently, "you should be glad to have some one buy the vineyard from the Vicomte. His character is not so good. First of all, he is in debt, deeply involved. He cannot pay. Secondly, he is a *bon vivant*. He loves his wine, his women. He is a spendthrift. He is tempted—and who knows when his temptation will be stronger than he is? Moreover, he cannot be civil to his nephew, who comes all the way from England to befriend him. And do you know why? In the midst of all his troubles, he finds time to pursue Madame Fürst. But Madame is no fool. She sees he is an empty cask. She will have nothing to do with him. She is expensive, Madame; she must have a man of money, she is not for bankrupts. And so he lures her into his wine-room and destroys her."

"You accuse him?"

"The facts accuse him," said Fugger Bey. "What else could have happened? This man, Marty—is he the type to commit a crime of passion? I do not think so. He is a blunt, stupid fellow. He loves his wine, his women, and a song, no doubt—but how? He gulps his wine, he tumbles his women, he bawls his songs at the top of his voice. He has no discrimination. He is not the man to involve himself about any particular woman, much less a woman like Madame Fürst.

"But this Vicomte, this Frenchman, where is he? He drove away, you will say, to Bordeaux. He is gone already one or two hours before Madame is killed. But I would call your attention, Mr. Congreve, to this little fact. If one can drive *towards* Bordeaux, one can also drive *back* again.

"The Vicomte has arranged a little trap for you, my friend. He has fooled you. But he cannot so easily deceive me. You Americans are so trusting. You allow the Frenchmen to pull the wool over your eyes too easily. But we Germans, we have lived beside them. We have watched them for a long, long time. We know what they are. Ach, if you will look a little deeper, you will find that I am right. This is a crime of passion. Why else should any one attack Madame Fürst? Poor Natalie!"

"Why do you tell me all this?" Congreve asked, as if at a loss to understand.

"Surely you do not imagine that I am so dull as not to know that I, also, am a suspect in this case," the Bey explained. "It was I who left the dinner table with Madame. I was the last man seen with her before she was murdered. You can hardly blame me for refusing to be inconvenienced in order to let the murderer escape."

"Ah," said Congreve, "go on. What were your relations with Madame Fürst?"

"We were on the best of terms," said the Bey complacently, taking another sip of the golden Montrachet. "Madame is no fool.

She knew that the Vicomte had no future. She had amused herself with this Englishman also—but only to pass the time."

"And Arno?" Congreve queried.

"Ah, *that* is the point," said Fugger Bey, nodding. "*That* is it. For me, she had real liking. We understood each other. But Arno, though rich, is not sympathetic. You saw how he behaved to Madame just before she went off with me."

"Where did you go?"

"When we left the table, we got our coats and went immediately to the gateway of the Château. There was Arno's taxi. I knew it was there, for I had come with him in it and had heard him tell the man to wait. Arno has always a taxi waiting, wherever he goes. A folly, but he can afford it.

"Just as we reached the taxi, Madame began to reproach me for defending her against Arno. You will understand, of course, I could not endure *that*. I had acted in her interest—jeopardized my future and my position for her sake—yet no sooner had I saved her from the man's insults than she turned on me and scolded me. Naturally, I was enraged; I was furious. I beat her."

"You beat her?"

"Certainly I beat her. She squealed and struggled. But I struck her two or three times in the face. I could have strangled her!"

"Go on," said Congreve.

"I could have strangled her, I tell you. She deserved it, I thought, at that moment, for forgetting my affection. Am I to be scolded for a-a-an American business man? Me? Fugger Bey! Of course I beat her. But she turned and ran from me back through the gates towards the Château, leaving her cloak on the ground. I ran after her for a few steps. Then I was angry. I thought, 'No, let her go back to Arno if she will, the fool.' I waited thereby the taxi."

"The taxi driver witnessed all this, I suppose?"

"Yes, certainly," said the Bey. "That is why I am telling you. I have brought the man here to verify my statement. He will tell you that everything happened as I say."

"Splendid! And then?" Congreve prompted.

"Well, then I relented," said the Bey. "I followed her. She went up to the top of the court yard and under the archway. The moon was bright and I could see her white dress. There was a light in the Englishman's room. I supposed she might be going back to him again. Monkhouse did not understand Madame Fürst. He was too easy on the woman. So, after a time, I followed her, keeping in the shadow of the wall, up the slope. But when I reached the *chai* door, I heard voices inside. One of those voices was hers."

"Ah," said Congreve, "and the other voices?"

The Bey shrugged.

"It was French they were speaking, that is certain," he said. "Well, then I tried to open the door. I could see a light through the keyhole, but the door was locked. So I waited, hoping she would come out—not quite sure what I should do. If I had called to her, she wouldn't have come, after what had just happened, so I said nothing. Perhaps, if I had called out or knocked at the door, Natalie might have been spared. Then some one came out into the moonlight on the other side of the courtyard, and I decided I had better not be found there.

"I went back through the shadows to the car. The taxi took me to the hotel in the village. There I remained until Monkhouse, on his way to Bordeaux, brought me news of the murder. I was very unhappy. But after a time, I decided to come back and let you know what had happened. I was the last man seen with Madame, I confess it. I quarreled with her. But I am *not* the man who killed her."

"Do you happen to know any one by the name of Percy?" Congreve asked.

"That is an English name, isn't it?" said the German, looking blank.

"Or Daniel? Marty says that Madame called out in the *chai*, 'Daniel, oh, Daniel.'"

"Ah," said the Bey, smiling and nodding with evident pleasure. "She remembered me then. But your man Marty did not hear her correctly. The name she called was undoubtedly Danilo. That is the name of the Prince in the light opera, 'The Merry Widow,' you recall. Natalie was always romantic."

"And you, then, are Danilo?" said Congreve.

The Bey smirked with sentimental satisfaction.

"*I* am Danilo," he replied. "So she remembered me, at the last?"

Congreve shook his head. "Unfortunately, not at the last. She called for Danilo when she first came into the *chai*."

"But," said the Bey, starting up, "that is impossible. She had left me outside. She would not have looked for me in the *chai*. I was outside, I tell you. I was not there."

"I am afraid," said Congreve, "that remains to be proved. I must ask you to remain in the Château, at least until after luncheon."

Fugger Bey bowed.

Congreve turned to me.

"Merton," he said, "would you mind checking up on the Bey's story with the taximan?"

"Not at all," I replied, and went out.

Fifteen minutes later, I made my report to Congreve. He was alone.

"The taxi driver," I announced, "tells a story which checks in every way with that of the Bey, except in one respect. The Bey did not return to the inn in the taxi. The driver's passenger was Arno."

"Ah," said Congreve, "I fear the Bey's tip to the taxi driver was not large enough."

"Did you learn anything more from the Bey while I was gone?" I asked him.

"A little," Congreve replied. "It appears that Arno has bargained, not only for Château Roet, but also for the extensive Algerian vineyards belonging to the Vicomte. I happen to know that the wine produced in those Algerian vineyards is of very inferior quality. Does this suggest anything to you?"

"I am afraid not," I confessed,

"Indeed!" said Congreve. "It occurs to me that the Bey has deceived us in more than one detail of his little story. What do we know of Arno's real purpose in buying this vineyard? It seems unlikely that he intends to go into business here. How could the vineyard of Château Roet be expanded? Château Roet is so tiny; you know the vintage here seldom exceeds twenty-five barrels. Every available yard of these hills is already occupied by vineyards almost equally celebrated. There is no direction in which he could expand. How, then, can he hope to produce vast quantities of wine here for export?"

"I give up," I said.

"There's only one method," Congreve went on. "Arno might follow the method he used in the States in manufacturing bootleg liquor."

"You mean he would adulterate Château Roet?" I was horrified.

"Why not?" said Congreve. "Such a plan would strike a man of his type as excellent. It is just what he has been used to. Not many of the Algerian wines are well enough known to be much in demand, but it would be a simple matter to ship such cheap wines to the States, and by a little chemical trickery and blending, palm them off on the American market as genuine Château Roet. As owner of the vineyard, Arno could probably evade detection for a long time. We must not forget that very few Americans have had our opportunity to cultivate a taste for vintage wines during recent years. By the time the great American public is capable of discrimination in such matters, our friend, Arno, will have salted away a million dollars."

"It's an outrage," I declared hotly.

"Of course it is an outrage. But until the United States Government takes steps to guard against adulteration and misrepresentation, such enterprises are bound to be undertaken, and Goosey Rauh, alias Mr. Everett Arno, is just the man to undertake them. Every one knows that in the States he was engaged in illegal traffic in narcotics. He is merely attempting to combine the liquor racket with his old racket in drugs."

"Do you suppose Monkhouse is in on this deal?" I demanded. "He brought Arno here to buy the vineyard."

"It is hard to say," said Congreve. "He might have been taken in. Englishmen as a race are a singularly unsuspicious breed."

"Monkhouse doesn't strike me as in great need of money," I suggested. "That mistress of his looked terribly expensive. He dresses well, and his car must have cost a pretty penny. Of course, he may have been squeezing the Vicomte out of personal spite. He made no pretense of loving his uncle."

"Yes," said Congreve, "that was frank. Still, for all that, we must not overlook the fact that your Englishman specializes in public virtue. While he would not betray his country or accept a bribe in public office, he might be less particular in personal affairs."

"Say!" I cried, struck by a sudden thought. "This Englishman is interested in chemicals, too."

"Yes," said Congreve indifferently, "that is true. But the thing that puzzles me is *why* did Madame Fürst turn against the Bey after they left the Château last night? Why should she scold *him?*"

"Ask the Bey," I suggested.

"I tried that," said Congreve dryly.

"What did he say?"

"He insisted it was a private matter—nothing to do with me or my little investigation. I think he was afraid to talk."

"Where is he now?"

"Upstairs. I persuaded him to remain until after lunch to-morrow."

CHAPTER X
THE EVIDENCE OF M. LE VICOMTE

WE TWO SAT ON, in the *salon*.

As the night wore on, Congreve's spirits seemed to fall lower and lower, and at the end of that interview, a cloud seemed to settle upon him. I commented on it.

"Don't be discouraged, George," I urged. "You've uncovered a great deal, you know. You're getting on with it. Never say die."

"You think I appear discouraged?" he asked sadly. "I'm not, I assure you—only depressed. It is distressing to consider the possibility that a friend could be a murderer. Yet one must be honest and face the possibilities."

"Probabilities, rather," I amended his phrase. "Nearly everything you turn up seems to point to the Vicomte. But after all, we must try to look at this from the point of view of the French. They make great allowances for a crime of passion. Is it so surprising that a man like the Vicomte, so susceptible, so gallant, so self-indulgent, should lose his head and resort to violence when he finds himself rejected by the woman he desires? If he did not murder her, why did he skip out? Where is he now?"

"Wherever he is," said George, "it seems pretty certain that he did *not* go to Bordeaux. He must have had a plan of some sort."

"It looks to me," I threw in, "as if he had arranged the whole matter in advance. He was evidently quite annoyed with Madame Fürst in the *chai*, yet later he invited her to dinner and to lunch tomorrow in the most affable manner. It seems probable that he made an assignation with her in the Bureau. She went to him there, calling his name. She used his keys to open the door."

"I suppose she did," said Congreve. "But if he asked her to come to the Bureau during dinner . . ."

"Dinner was delayed, you remember," I reminded him. "Probably that was why she left early. She certainly got rid of the Bey in short order."

"Yes," said Congreve, "so she did. You may be right."

"It seems odd, though," I offered, "that she should have to pick Monkhouse's pocket to get the key of the Bureau, if the Vicomte had invited her there. The Vicomte had his own keys, certainly. Why didn't he give them to her, if he wanted her to join him?"

"That seems a point in his favor," said Congreve, "but I'm afraid it has no validity."

"Why not?" I asked.

"Well," he said, "that's Monkhouse's story. But I know Eugéne. It's hard to believe that he gave his nephew a key. The story is too thin. I don't believe it. Under pressure, he might give Monkhouse a key to the cellar, but surely *not* a key to the Bureau."

"Perhaps the Vicomte left his keys in the door of the Bureau for Madame's convenience," I suggested. "You remember Lewin recognized that key ring as the Vicomte's."

"That is more likely," Congreve assented. "But it all seems so cold-blooded, for a crime of passion. The Vicomte was in high spirits when he left us, that is clear. Arno had solved his financial problems. And Madame Fürst was a realist in her way. She was not the sort of sentimental fool who goes to visit a jilted lover in order to inform him that she is through. *That* strikes me as utterly out of character. If then, he desired her, if she was complaisant, and if all other obstacles were removed, what becomes of our crime of passion?"

"'All men are liars,'" I quoted.

"Pah!" Congreve got up, disgusted. "Now I've done it! This bottle has 'gone off.' I'll never be able to think this through now!"

"Bosh," I protested. "Try another. Ask some more questions."

"Merton," Congreve said, "I've asked questions until everybody is sick of me, and still no solution."

"No proof, you mean," I offered. "The solution is clear enough to me."

"Not really?" Congreve countered.

"Yes, really, Congreve," I said sleepily. "There are a lot of things not proved, which are, nevertheless, obvious. The Vicomte *is* the guilty man."

"Ah, yes," said Congreve dully. "What was the motive?"

"Damn the motive," I said. "We all have scores of motives never acted upon. Does a Frenchman have to have a motive? Do you have to look far for a motive when a passionate old roué wants to get rid of an avid, unscrupulous mistress? It is plain as mud. The Vicomte drove away towards Bordeaux. At the first opportunity, he ditches his chauffeur, hires or borrows a car, and comes back, having first made an assignation with Madame and given her the key to the Bureau. She comes, impelled by the novelty of his plea, or for some reason best known to herself. He gets rid of her, skips out the back door, hops over the wall, piles into his car, and is gone. He has a perfect alibi. And you have your trouble for nothing."

"Very interesting," said Congreve, "and I don't say the theory has no possibilities; but it is hardly convincing to me."

"Well what's *your* solution?"

"My dear fellow, I have no solution. If the Vicomte is guilty, the Vicomte is the guilty man. If not, we can only rely upon our trusted old stand-bys—the first, second, and third murderers. Your first suggestion, you remember, Merton."

"Well, what do you intend to do, then?" I demanded, surly with fatigue.

"There's only one thing more I can do that occurs to me at the moment, Merton. I don't know about murderers, but detectives always revisit the scene of the crime. It occurs to me that if you and I and the *maître de chai* should do just that thing, we might perhaps hit upon some clue which would keep us going until our friend, the Vicomte, turns up."

"He'll never turn up here," I said doggedly.

"But why not? You just insisted he had a perfect alibi."

"Well," I sneered sourly, "he's probably afraid to return because *you* are sleuthing on the case."

Congreve laughed good-humoredly. "Run along and call in the good *maître*, Merton. A bit of fresh air will do you a world of good."

"All right," I agreed, and heaved myself up out of my chair. "That last idea is the best you've had so far."

I found the *maître de chai* hovering around the building, patrolling the path from one door to another, and together we went back to find Congreve. He appeared to be in better humor. The three of us immediately set out for the *chai*. Congreve suggested that we enter by the courtyard door.

"There is no necessity for going through the Bureau this time," he said.

For my part, I was glad of that.

With a hammer, the *maître* removed the nails which held the door, then unlocked it with his key. He lighted three candles. Then we all went down the staircase. The Gascon went first; I followed; and Congreve came last. I had already reached the bottom, where the Gascon muttered profanely over the ruins of the empty hogshead and lamented the loss of so many liters of that priceless vintage, when I discovered that Congreve was still above, bent over, inspecting the edge of the unrailed steps. He was making noises indicating satisfaction, and I knew that one of his suspicions had been confirmed by something he found there.

"What is it?" I called up to him.

"Just as I thought," he said cheerily. "Madame was not thrown into the hogshead. She fell at the top of the steps and slithered down, leaving them just in time to slide headfirst into the vat. That's why Marty heard no splash, such as would have been audible if she had fallen from the landing above. It is evident, therefore, that the criminal had no intention of drowning her or concealing her body in the hogshead. He must have struck her without any premeditated plan, in a moment of passion. He had no time to dispose of the body or to make plans for the disposal of it, because of the noise Marty made just then. All he could do was to put out the light and run for it. You can see tiny shreds of Madame's costume caught on the steps."

He came on down and joined the two of us on the earthen floor. "What a mess," he said.

The whole place smelled horribly of must and the earth was still sticky and damp with wine. The mallet with which the murder had been done lay on the floor.

We moved on under the gallery where the cooper's materials were stored. Two or three barrels, in various stages of completion, stood on the earthen floor. Over one of these, the *maître's* blue blouse hung limp. The floor here was dry.

Moving out from under the gallery again, we followed Congreve down the aisle to the barrel on which we had found the body of Madame Fürst. The *maître* grumbled, and would have rolled it back into its place, at the head of the row. The new cask, heavy with wine, resisted his efforts, and a moment later Congreve was there, protesting.

"Nothing must be moved," he said.

The Gascon resented Congreve's interference, but desisted, and went grumbling back to the head of the row, where the stray cask should have been. Once there, he halted, and uttered an oath. We two hurried up to join him.

"What is the matter?" Congreve demanded.

"Nothing, but nothing," the Gascon replied. "Only it seems this cask is not in position. It is not where it lay when I saw it last."

"Can it be," Congreve demanded, "that some one has been in here? Have you sealed the doors properly? Have you kept guard?"

The Gascon evidently resented these suspicions.

"I am certain, Monsieur," he replied. "No one can have entered here. And see, the earth is all soaked with wine, yet there are no fresh tracks. No one can have disturbed this barrel."

"Then how can it have moved?" Congreve demanded.

"Who knows?" said the *maître*. "Perhaps I was mistaken."

"Not likely you'd be mistaken about one of your own barrels, is it?" Congreve demanded.

"Not likely, but possible," the Gascon replied stubbornly.

Congreve bent over the new cask and inspected it. It was just like all the others in that end of the row, so far as I could see, but he seemed to find it interesting.

"Look here, Merton," he said suddenly. "The earth is still very wet under this cask. It is leaking, or rather, it has been leaking."

The Gascon came bustling up to see.

"*Un tonneau percé?*" he questioned. "*Impossible!*"

But on inspection, he had to admit that such an error had been made. Whereupon he began to curse the cooper volubly.

"Yes, there is a leak," he said. "You can see, here is the crack. The man is too old for his work."

He attempted to roll the cask over, but Congreve seized his arm.

"Wait," he said. "Where is this leak?"

"Here on the top," the *maître* declared irritably, holding the candle close.

"Odd," said Congreve, "that it should leak from the top."

The Gascon stood up suddenly, as though he had been stuck with a pin behind. Then he bent to look again.

"You are right, Monsieur," he said, "There is no other leak."

He rocked the keg gently. There was no sound of sloshing wine.

"It is empty," he said sadly. "What would M. le Vicomte say?"

The Gascon seized the cask to carry it back under the gallery, but to my surprise the man, strong as he was, failed in his attempt. The cask was too much for him and resisted his strength.

Suddenly he cried out, "There is something strange here. This is not one of my casks. That one in the aisle there should be here. This one does not belong."

He ran under the gallery and picked up a hammer. With this, in a few moments, his practiced hand knocked the hoops from the barrel. The end of it fell out. Then the Gascon sprang back with a cry. A man's legs showed in the opened cask. Instantly Congreve sprang forward, and taking the hammer from the hand of the astonished Gascon, completed his work. The barrel fell to pieces—the whole figure lay revealed. Gingerly Congreve took hold of the bedraggled coat and turned the body over. The pale face of the Vicomte shone in the light of my candle.

CHAPTER XI
THE EVIDENCE OF MR. LEWIN

WHEN THE VICOMTE'S body was revealed, the emotion of the old
Gascon was painful to witness. He seemed entirely overwhelmed,
and though he made heroic efforts to control himself, the tears
streamed down his weather-beaten face.

Congreve and I were embarrassed by his show of feeling and
busied ourselves examining the body. I suspected that Congreve
could not trust his own voice at that moment; he and the Vicomte
had shared too many grand bottles together.

The body was hatless, but otherwise dressed just as we had last
seen the living man. His hat, crushed and saturated with wine, lay
in the cask near his head. Congreve lifted it, and immediately I
saw the glint of gold in the dark lees. I recognized the Vicomte's
old-fashioned gold watch. Congreve picked it up. The case was
slightly dented and the lid sprung open, the crystal shattered. The
hands pointed to seven twenty-six.

Laying the hat and watch aside, Congreve asked me to help him
with the body. We laid it out upon the casks, and immediately
Congreve began his inspection.

"Look here, Merton," he said, "Eugéne was killed with the same
mallet which destroyed Madame. See, here on the back of the head,
is the mark of it. He must have been hit a terrific blow from behind. It would seem as though he must have been stooping when
he was struck."

I was quite willing to take Congreve's word for these details,
for the Vicomte, pale and slimy with must, his whole clothing saturated with fermenting juice of the grape, was a sickening spectacle.

But Congreve's love of his friend seemed to make him unconscious of these circumstances. Methodically, he proceeded to search the dead man's pockets. His labor went almost unrewarded. There were no keys, of course. That was to be expected, for the Vicomte's keys had been found in the door of the Bureau. There was no cash on the body. That, to me, seemed a strange circumstance, for, hard up though the Vicomte was, it seemed unnatural that a Frenchman of his rank should have no money whatever on his person, in a country where bank checks are so little used. From the inner pocket of his coat, Congreve brought out a brown leather wallet. But there was no money even in that. Only a memorandum of some social engagement and a folded slip of paper.

Unfolding this, Congreve studied it, and looked up at me significantly.

"Merton," he said, "look at this. This is interesting."

All my time in France has never made me accustomed to French penmanship, and the script on this slip of paper was rendered almost illegible by the soaking and discoloration it had got in the cask.

"Explain," I said. "I can't make it out."

"No," he said. "It is difficult. That's just the point. It was written recently. The ink is almost entirely washed out. Nevertheless, it is a puzzling document."

"Explain," I repeated.

"This," he said, "is a receipt for one hundred thousand francs, dated yesterday, issued to the Vicomte and signed by Bertrand Monkhouse."

"Then," I said, "the Englishman was lying to us all the time."

"On the contrary," Congreve corrected me, "his story is verified in that the Vicomte evidently paid his debt or some part of it immediately before starting to Bordeaux. But where the devil do you suppose he got one hundred thousand francs?"

We were interrupted by the *maître de chai*, who had now found his tongue again. He addressed Congreve with great emotion.

"Ah, Monsieur," he said, "I have wronged him. I supposed he might have done this murder, and I have wronged you too, Monsieur, and tried to mislead you. But now I would that you forgive me. I will help you. We will catch the murderer. We will send him to the guillotine, whoever he is. Command me, Monsieur. I am at your service."

"Good," said Congreve. "Call some one whom you can trust and carry the Vicomte into his bedroom. Afterward, I have an errand or two for you."

The Gascon assented with alacrity.

Congreve and I left him. Going slowly up the steps, we came out into the dark courtyard. I was glad to be in the fresh air.

"Where did Eugéne get that money?" said Congreve softly, as though talking to himself. "Do you suppose Madame Fürst knew that he had it? If so, her going to the Bureau after him is reasonable enough. She had always an eye to the main chance, and with his keys might have gone there looking for him."

"Surely," I objected, "if she expected him there, she would never have rifled the safe, as she seems to have done."

"If she went into the Bureau," Congreve continued, "she must have heard the thumping of the cooper at work, just as Marty did. That would have lured her on into the *chai*. It is the only explanation I can think of for her going into the *chai* at that time of night. No wonder she feared Arno, if she knew that the Vicomte was able to pay his debt and avoid the sale of the vineyard. She would hardly have looted the safe if she had expected to find the Vicomte there. Let's go in and consult Arno."

In the *salon* we found Lewin, fretting. He demanded what we had been doing and was thunderstruck by our revelation. For once, Lewin had nothing to say. He was evidently waiting for Congreve to make the first move.

Congreve had brought along the mallet and offered it to Lewin. But he wouldn't touch it, and George laid it down.

"Everything," said Congreve, "will have to be reconsidered now. It seemed impossible from the first that Eugéne could have been guilty of the murder. The condition of his body and the time at which his watch was stopped puts that beyond all doubt. He was dead long before Madame went into the *chai*."

"No doubt she interrupted the murder and was silenced there," I suggested.

"How can you tell?" Lewin broke in, "It doesn't follow that the same party committed both crimes."

"Right," said Congreve. "I was coming to that. But Madame certainly did not interrupt the murder of the Vicomte. His watch was stopped at seven twenty-six. If Marty's story is true, she was killed about ten-twenty. Even if Marty was lying, we know she left the table after nine-thirty. Nevertheless, it does seem reasonable to believe that these two murders have some connection."

"Well, then," said Lewin, "let's go over this and decide what must be done."

"Sorry, Lewin," said Congreve, and I was startled at the new gravity in his voice. "I'm afraid that from now on I must ask you to withdraw from our deliberations."

"Why, what's the matter?" Lewin interrupted. "I'm not entirely useless, I hope. Besides, I'm your employer. You can't leave me out. I suggested this."

"I know you did," Congreve agreed heavily, "and I regret that circumstances compel me to break off our relationship. The job you gave me was both pleasant and profitable. But Eugéne was my friend. I intend to carry this investigation through to a finish. Surely you can see that I cannot accept your pay, Lewin, while working on a case in which you yourself are a suspect."

"Well, I'm damned," said Lewin. His face grew red. "You've got the nerve of a brass monkey. From the start, I have done what I could to help and pointed out the weakness in every man's story."

Congreve interrupted. "I noticed that and I wondered why."

"I should think that's plain enough," Lewin countered quickly. "I want this thing settled. I want the guilty one caught. I want to get out of this and get on with my trip. But if you don't want me to talk, have it your own way, and be damned."

"I do want you to talk, Lewin," said Congreve. "I do. Never doubt that. What's more, I want you to tell something. All along you have simply tried to throw dust in my eyes. You've been too anxious to hang this crime on somebody else. Now it is time for you to tell us what you know. You've kept a great deal back, Lewin, you know you have."

"Nothing important, nothing useful," Lewin defended himself.

"I can judge better of that when I've heard what you know," Congreve commented dryly. "But I've found out some things about you without your help—some things that may make it hard for you if the police take up this investigation, as they must do very soon."

"That's it," said Lewin. "That's why—"

Congreve interrupted. "What business were you in, in the States?"

"Oil," said Lewin. "I made my money in the Oklahoma oil fields."

"And before that?"

"Oh, I was engaged in various enterprises," Lewin explained vaguely. "I tried my hand at several things—sort of a jack-of-all-trades you might say."

"This sort of talk isn't helping you any, Lewin," Congreve declared sternly. "You manufactured barrels at one time, I believe?"

"For a while, yes. It was only a small concern. I soon got rid of it."

"How long were you in that business?"

"Two, three years," said Lewin. "That was a long time ago."

"How many men did you employ?"

"Oh, at first, only two."

"You worked in the shop yourself?"

"Yes, at first."

"As a cooper?" Congreve demanded.

"Yes," Lewin admitted.

"Were you a good cooper?"

"Good enough. I sold my barrels. I had no complaints. I made money and sold out at a profit." Lewin seemed puzzled by Congreve's questioning. "What's all this got to do with your investigation?"

"I should think that is obvious enough," Congreve explained wearily. "At any rate, the connection will be sufficiently clear to the French police. The body of the Vicomte was found in a barrel. Somebody put it there—somebody who knew how to make barrels."

"The barrel was ready-made," Lewin countered. "You must have seen that yourself."

"Not completely made," Congreve objected. "The barrelhead had to be put in and made tight, after the body was placed in the cask. That must have been done by a man who had some skill as a cooper. You had that skill. I'm afraid that unless you can help us find some one else guilty, you are in for a bad time of it, Lewin."

The color drained from Lewin's face. His cheeks went flabby. He stepped unsteadily to a chair and sat down. At that moment, he looked pathetically like a small boy about to receive a whipping.

"All right," he sighed. "I'll talk."

"Good," said Congreve. "I'm sure you can help a great deal. But first, I think a drink would do you good."

For a moment Lewin stiffened.

"Going to make a guinea pig out of me too, are you?" he grumbled.

"Yes," said Congreve. "I shall prescribe for you too. I suppose you'd like a sweet Sauterne—again," he continued, ostentatiously looking at the wine stain on Lewin's waistcoat.

Slowly the meaning of his glance dawned upon the disturbed old gentleman.

"Why do you say sweet Sauterne, man?" he demanded.

"That's a sweet Sauterne on your waistcoat, isn't it, Lewin?" Congreve asked.

"Good Lord," said Lewin. "You're a wizard. How did you know that?"

"I have my skill too," said Congreve, "just as you have a knack for making barrels—and money. But this time I sha'n't give you a sweet Sauterne. It's a little too cloying, too soothing. You need something to brace and clarify your memory. You're going to tell me all you know. The whole truth this time. That's agreed?"

"You bet," said Lewin. "Go ahead and prescribe."

We all relaxed a little.

"Merton," he suggested, "do you mind bringing over that bottle of Cheval Blanc from the buffet? I think it will fill the bill nicely. And please don't shake the bottle, Merton. You're altogether too careless in such matters."

I brought the designated bottle carefully from the buffet. He opened it skillfully. He whiffed the cork, and his face showed approval. Having poured a little into his own glass, he helped each of us in turn, and when the wine had been drunk, he set his glass down upon the table and leaned back in his chair.

"All right, Lewin," he said. "I want a complete account of your movements and your doings from the time you went down into the cellar until dinner."

"Well, Mr. Congreve," said Lewin, without raising his eyes to meet Congreve's glance. "I'm afraid that story I told you about buying the cellar from the Vicomte wasn't strictly true."

"I suspected as much," said Congreve dryly.

"You see," Lewin went on, "I'm not a man to advertise what I'm up to. I figure that my business is mine and nobody else's. As Confucius says: 'A wise man acts first and speaks afterward, according to his actions.' That's my rule, and it's a good one. After all, you and Merton are comparative strangers to me. My wife don't approve of my drinking. Marty is a sot who will blab all he knows in his cups, and this Miss Simpson is little better than a half-wit. No sensible man in my situation could afford to tell all he knows.

"Well, the fact is, when the Vicomte took me down in that cellar, and I found myself surrounded by all those thousands of bottles of fine wines, I talked turkey to him. I wanted him alone. That was why I first suggested that he and I should go down there together and the rest of you stay outside. I had to have an excuse for that, and a test of your skill was my excuse. I suppose you thought that was funny at the time. I'd already hired you and put the money on the barrelhead. If I hadn't been sure you knew your business, I never would have taken you on. You spotted that, I suppose?"

Congreve shifted uneasily. "To tell you the truth, Lewin, you fooled me completely. I thought it perfectly natural that you should wish to test my connoisseurship. My little vanity in such matters blinded me, I suppose."

"Well, anyhow, that was how I figured it," said Lewin. "But my real object in going down in that cellar with the Vicomte was not what you thought. I knew the Vicomte needed money. He told us so himself. I didn't know who his creditors were then and didn't care. I didn't know what Mr. Arno, as he calls himself, was up to.

But I believed that Butch Marty was telling the truth about Arno. And I thought that if I told the Vicomte that his buyer was a big-shot bootlegger and crook, he would refuse to sell the vineyard to him. Of course, I had heard the Vicomte say that he wouldn't give good wine to people who were not fit to appreciate it, and there was just a chance that he wouldn't mind cheating the American public, the same as Goosey did. He might consider that he was justified in taking advantage of those whose education in fine wines was interrupted, or prevented, by Prohibition. But even if the Vicomte was willing to cheat the American public, I figured he would fight shy of doing business with a crook like Goosey Rauh. So when I got down there alone with him, I put it straight to him. In confidence—of course. That's why I couldn't tell you the truth about it until I knew he was dead.

"Well, he jumped a mile high, like I expected he would. Said he was ruined either way. I let him get all hot and bothered for a while, until he was ripe and ready for some one to step in and talk business. Then I stepped in and offered to take care of his liabilities and put him on his feet again for a share in the vineyard and enough of his cellar to make me happy for the rest of my life.

"I'll say this for the Vicomte. He knows his own mind. It didn't take him five minutes to shake hands on that deal. He kissed me on both cheeks so hard that I figured I must have got stung on the deal. But after all, I have only got so many years to live and it would be a great comfort to have a cellar full of bottles you can rely on and be a partner in one of the greatest vineyards in France. I've got no children. The only kick I get out of life now I get out of a bottle, and believe me, I want it to be a good bottle every time."

"And then," Congreve prompted.

"Well, I put the money in his hand."

"You gave him a check?" Congreve asked.

"Check nothing," said Lewin. "I don't bother with checks over here. In these times, you can't take chances on checks and letters of credit. You want your money in currency. Then no matter what happens, you're safe over here."

"And what was the amount you paid over?"

"One hundred thousand francs I paid down," Lewin explained.

"You mean you had on you one hundred thousand francs in currency?" I cried, in amazement.

"Sure. That ain't such a lot of money. Of course it wasn't near enough, but I figured it was enough to clinch the deal, and believe me, I was glad to hand it over."

"No wonder you keep a bodyguard," I exclaimed.

"Well," said Lewin, "they were all bills of large denomination. Not such a big roll as you might think. So I paid him, and we fixed it all up. He was so excited that I had to make the plans. My idea was that he should go to Bordeaux just as he had told us he would, pay his creditors, and bring back the notary to make our deal legal. Of course I wasn't sure, but I thought it likely that if Arno was really Goosey Rauh, he might get ornery and make trouble, if he found out that I had stepped in and queered his game. You see, I believe in Butch.

"Of course, we had to keep everybody from suspecting what was up, so I told the Vicomte to throw a party and keep everybody here, just as if everything was running according to schedule. Then, when he got to Bordeaux, he was to notify the police and bring them back, so as to keep an eye on Goosey and, if necessary, run him out. That was the plan. Also I wanted to keep the whole business dark from Mamma. She'd have a fit if she knew I was going into the liquor business, as she calls it. So the Vicomte agreed that I should be a silent partner in the business. That was why everything had to be confidential. The Vicomte saw the sense of that and everything was settled to my satisfaction.

"Then he picked out a few bottles, and we came upstairs again. I guess the old Gascon knew that something was up, but, of course, he didn't know what, for I have to do my talking in English, and I stuck too close to the Vicomte to give him a chance to tell anything to the *maître de chai*. It was all settled in ten or fifteen minutes. Then we came out of the cellar, got rid of the bottles, and went on over to the Vicomte's office."

"Why did you go with him there?" asked Congreve.

"To get a receipt, of course. I hope you don't think I'm the kind of a sap who would hand over six thousand dollars in secret and take no receipt?"

"You have the receipt, I suppose?" Congreve asked.

Lewin thrust his hand into the breast pocket of his coat, brought out a shiny leather wallet, produced a folded slip of paper, and laid it on the table before Congreve.

"There it is," he said. "Of course, it's only a memorandum receipt, unstamped, and maybe not legal, but it was all I required, or could get at the time. I've done a good deal of business in my day, and the Vicomte struck me as a man of his word."

Congreve studied the receipt.

"It seems genuine," he said, nodding. "It is Eugéne's signature, undoubtedly."

"You bet it's genuine," said Lewin, now more cheerful. "He gave it to me, and I put it in my pocket. Just then, this Englishman, Monkhouse, came trotting down the stairs and looked in at the office door. That was where the Vicomte made his first mistake, I guess. That roll of bills was lying on his desk in plain sight, and the Englishman spotted it the first thing. For a minute, he stood there, looking in, then stepped inside, sucking away on his pipe; but never said a word. I guess he saw what had happened. Anyhow, the Vicomte acted as if the secret was out—not that he seemed to think it mattered much. Maybe he was glad to see his nephew. He seemed to be feeling mighty good. At any rate, he told Monkhouse that he was ready to settle, and asked him to sign a receipt and surrender the notes he held. The Englishman signed, and said he would go up to his room and get the notes. The Vicomte said it didn't matter; that he was in a hurry.

"Just then we heard somebody's shoes on the gravel outside. Monkhouse walked out. It was a good thing he did, too, for just then this fellow, Arno, stuck his head in the door, and right after him came the Bey. It seems that Arno had counted on going to Bordeaux with the Vicomte. He didn't cotton to the idea of hanging around the Château for twenty-four hours in the company of Butch Marty and a lot of other, Americans, I judge. He kept telling the Vicomte he wanted to go with him and settle the deal immediately. So the Vicomte had to talk him out of it.

"Well, my business was settled, and I didn't see that my staying there was going to help matters any. I was afraid Arno would catch on to what was up if I showed too much interest. So I said good-by and left the office."

"When you left the Vicomte," Congreve demanded, "both Arno and the Bey were in the office with him?"

"That's right," said Lewin, "both of them. And the Englishman was expected downstairs any minute. But I guess the Vicomte thought he wouldn't wait for Monkhouse. He was having a hard time getting rid of Arno and the Dutchman. At any rate, he locked up his safe, took his brief case, got into the car, and slammed the door. But Arno and the Bey wouldn't stop talking. They kept after him and followed him out to the car and talked to him through the window. Maybe you heard the car door slam?"

Both Congreve and I nodded.

"Well, that's the last I saw of the Vicomte," said Lewin. "I came out and joined you. It was just seven-twenty. We all saw the car drive off not ten minutes later.

"Then I went up to dress for dinner. On my way upstairs, I stepped into the dining room and got a bottle of sweet Sauterne, and carried it up to my room. A conducted tour is all very well, but I thought it would be fun to try one bottle out in private. I'd bought that cellar, or part of it, so I figured I wasn't stealing anything. Like a fool, I dressed for dinner before I opened the bottle, and when I pulled the cork, some of the wine was spilled on my clothes. I didn't want to put on a business suit for dinner and have to ex-plain to Mamma. It wasn't much of a stain, so I let it go. That's how my waistcoat got the wine on it.

"That's all I know about this business.

"To tell the truth, I didn't like the way things were going any too well. If Arno and Goosey Rauh are the same man, a man as rich as I am isn't any too safe here. For all I knew, Arno might have guessed what was up and might take his revenge by kidnap-ping me. These underworld boys, they say, have connections all over the world. I figured that Arno might have confederates in Bordeaux, or maybe the Bey was one of his men.

"But how he could have murdered the Vicomte beats me. It wasn't ten minutes after the Vicomte slammed the door of the car till it drove through the courtyard under our very eyes.

"Of course, it may be that the Vicomte came back. But if that chauffeur told the truth, the car never stopped all the way to Bordeaux. If the time at which the Vicomte's watch stopped is the time of his death, he must have been tapped on the head while we were standing in the courtyard, waiting for the car to go.

"Now, I've made a clean breast of everything. I've told you the truth. That lets me out, I suppose?"

"Do you have any theory as to which of these men may have murdered the Vicomte?" Congreve demanded.

"Well," said Lewin thoughtfully, "it might have been one or two or all three of them. But if Marty's story is true, Arno is your man. You remember he said it was a man with black hair who tapped Madame Fürst on the head. And it looks as if the man who killed Madame Fürst did it because she caught him putting the Vicomte into the barrel. In that case, it was the same person, or persons, both times. There was money involved, and Goosey Rauh made his fortune killing people for money. Arno was with the Vicomte at the end, and the Bey belongs to Arno. Of course, Butch was drunk. He missed everything worth seeing, poor sot. I almost wish I had never hired him."

Congreve looked up curiously. "It does seem odd, Lewin, your hobnobbing with a fellow like Marty, if you don't mind my saying so."

Lewin's face was stricken, but he pulled himself together and said, in a strained voice, "I suppose it does, Mr. Congreve, but there's a reason. You see, Butch was my boy's buddy in the War. Dick didn't come back. Mamma and I have made it our business to look after Butch."

Congreve's voice was gentle. "I'm terribly sorry, Lewin."

Mr. Lewin evidently could not trust his voice. He smiled wryly and waved his hand as though brushing aside that memory.

"I guess I'll have another drink," he remarked irrelevantly.

We all lifted our glasses together, and though nothing was said, I sensed that we were all drinking to a sacred memory.

Lewin was first to break the silence. "If there's nothing more, Mr. Congreve, I think I'll go upstairs and see my wife."

PART THREE
THE SOLUTION

CHAPTER I
FIRST, SECOND AND THIRD MURDERERS

WHEN LEWIN HAD GONE, Congreve and I looked at each other for a time without speaking. Then my curiosity got the better of me.

"What do you think of Lewin's story, George?" I asked.

"Extremely interesting and extremely useful," he replied. "He raises many points of interest and simplifies our problem tremendously."

"For example," I said, "he knows how to make barrels, and the Vicomte's body was concealed in one."

"Yes," Congreve answered. "He was a cooper, undoubtedly."

"And a good one, by his own account," I said, hot on the trail. "No complaints—good barrels—made them himself."

"Yes," Congreve agreed, without enthusiasm. "He seemed proud of his work. He evidently made excellent barrels."

"He'll have a hard time explaining that away," I said.

"Do you think so?" said Congreve. "If he told us the truth, it's a great point in his favor. I only used it to scare him into talking."

"You don't think that counts against him?" I asked, in surprise.

"How could it?" said Congreve. "As you say, he made good barrels—barrels that did not leak. But the Vicomte was found in a leaky cask. The man who put him there was evidently no expert, or he would be there still."

"Ah," I said, "but the murderer was interrupted."

"No," said Congreve. "That's just the point. He was not interrupted until the Vicomte was safely in the cask and the cask had been filled with wine and put in place at the end of the row. The interruption occurred afterward."

147

"Well," I said, "it has been a long time since Lewin made casks."

"That is true," said Congreve, "but if he had had a hand in laying the Vicomte away, he would have seen the trend of my questioning, and would not have been so flabbergasted when I brought his skill as a cooper into the picture of the crime."

"He might have been acting," I persisted. "He's got a poker face."

"Precisely," said Congreve, "but it isn't the kind of acting such a man would offer at the moment of accusation. He could have had no motive for killing the Vicomte. Surely you never thought Lewin guilty?"

I stared at Congreve. "But you as good as accused him of the crime."

"Not at all," said Congreve. "I was merely annoyed with his secrecy and bored with his domineering interference. And so, of course, I frightened the truth out of him."

"All the same," I persisted, "it has been a long time since he made barrels, by his own account. If the cask leaked a little after a while, I think that fact is of small significance."

"Ah," said Congreve, "but it did not leak after a while. It leaked at once—and badly. So badly that it caused Madame Fürst to lose her life."

"Go on," I said. "This is too deep for me."

"Why," he said, "it's perfectly manifest. You know what the *maître* said—that the floor of the *chai* was normally dry. Yet Madame Fürst, running towards the stair—on her toes, mind you, as she must have been doing—slipped in the mud as she turned towards the stairway. Her slipper was muddy too, you remember. She had been in the *chai* only a few minutes. I would call your attention to the fact that it would take a considerable quantity of wine to make that hard earth floor muddy in such a short time. Therefore, the cask leaked badly from the first. In fact, it was her perception of the leak which probably caused her death."

"Explain," I said.

"It is perfectly clear. What language do you suppose she was speaking?"

"It is hard to say—German, probably, with the Bey; English or German with Arno; or English with Monkhouse or Lewin, maybe French, Roumanian, Hungarian, Italian—whatever you like."

"Marty said every word he heard was in English. 'Daniel dunno Percy.' What language do you suppose Marty knows?" Congreve demanded.

"English alone, I should think."

"Precisely. And when a man who knows only one language is listening, and makes out a phrase only now and then, what inference is to be drawn? It is to be supposed that the parties to the conversation changed suddenly from one language to another for his convenience? Hardly that, I think. Obviously what happened was that Marty turned into English those phrases that had English sounds. Obviously, 'Daniel dunno Percy' was *not* an English phrase, but one which *seemed* English to Marty's straining ears."

"But Marty said it was a man who uttered those words—a high squeaky voice."

"Precisely. There actually were three voices, as he said. But it does not follow that there were three speakers. One person may speak in more than one voice, as, for instance, in a state of high excitement. Madame Fürst was certainly in such a state of high excitement when she made her discovery."

"What discovery?" I demanded,

"The discovery of the leaky cask," Congreve explained. "The discovery that the Vicomte's body had been placed in it."

I listened, open-mouthed.

"She talked naturally enough with the murderer, whoever he was, until she realized that he was a murderer and that the body of his victim was in the cask. Then, naturally enough, she screamed. Madame Fürst was in the habit of raising her voice to a shrill pitch in moments of great excitement. You remember the Bey told us how she 'squealed' when he attacked her. It is a safe inference that Madame Fürst was, therefore, responsible for two of the three voices heard by Marty from his hiding-place."

"Go on," I said breathlessly.

"What language would she use, do you suppose?"

"Probably that which came natural to her, or that in which she was already conversing with the murderer."

"It may be," said Congreve. "We cannot tell, but I am convinced that she spoke French at that moment."

"Why?" I demanded.

"Because French is the only language I know in which the syllables she uttered could have a meaning in the circumstances. If she discovered the mud under the leaking cask and suspected the concealment of the Vicomte's body, or on the other hand, if she were informed of it by the murderer himself, what would she naturally say?"

"I give up," I said. "Go on and tell me."

"The only phrase I can think of which tallies with Marty's recollection of the syllables is *dans le tonneau percé*."

"*Dans le tonneau percé*," I echoed. "In the leaking cask!"

"Precisely," said Congreve. "When the murderer, or murderers, perceived that she guessed the secret, or that, having been informed of it, she would be no party to the crime, the change in their demeanor immediately made her realize that her life was in danger. Men who will kill once, will kill again. Madame unwisely screamed out her discovery and then wisely turned to fly. But the leaking cask, which had betrayed the murderer to her, also betrayed Madame. She slipped in the mud it had made. The murderer overtook her, and she met the same fate as the Vicomte."

"Then you think Madame had nothing to do with the original crime?" I queried.

"It seems quite unlikely, Merton," Congreve answered. "What was Madame? A gold digger. A woman whose attraction towards a man was in exact proportion to his wealth and generosity. Her whole philosophy of life, as shown by her conduct, was selfish and mercenary. Her desire was never to give, but always to take. She was not the woman to risk her little finger for a lover in danger of the guillotine. Her fickleness, her selfishness, her love of money prove that. It may be that the murderer himself informed her of his deed, in a mistaken belief that she would willingly shield him. Or it may be that she discovered or guessed what was going on. At any rate, she recoiled from the crime. Had she been allowed to go away, she might have betrayed the murderer at once or, what seems more likely, have blackmailed him mercilessly for the rest of his days. A lover foolish enough to tell her of his crime would regard her recoil as black treason. On the other hand, if he distrusted her already and she discovered his crime, his distrust would be magnified ten thousand times when she turned to escape. In either case, there was only one way to silence her. He took that way."

"Then you believe Marty's story?"

"In the main, I do. He had very little time to make it up. It checks in too many ways to be a complete fabrication. With some allowance for his drunken condition, I think we must accept his story. I, at least, am convinced that what happened is substantially what I have just outlined for you. She came into the *chai* looking for some one whom she called Danilo. Whoever it was she found there had just concealed the body of the Vicomte in the cask. That is clear. It seems almost certain that the man who had just concealed the body was the man who murdered the Vicomte. That is reasonable, surely."

"Quite," I agreed. "But there might have been two of them—or even three."

"There might have been. But even supposing that three men had had a hand in the murder of the Vicomte, it is unlikely in the extreme that all three of them would have gathered there to conceal the body. Either the ringleader or the actual murderer made that cask, or some one of his henchmen was forced to do it for him. I much prefer the first supposition."

"Whoever he was," I said, "he must have been a cool customer to postpone the concealment of the body until after dinner, if the murder was committed at the hour when the Vicomte's watch stopped."

"He was a cool customer. A very cool customer," Congreve agreed. "This bottle is serving you better than the others, Merton."

"Where do you suppose the body was all that time?" I demanded, ignoring his gibe.

"In the cask," said Congreve. "The leak in the cask, you remember, was at the end of the barrel, where the Vicomte's feet rested.

Now the *maître de chai* and the Vicomte both took great pride in their vineyard; their cooper must have been an expert in his work. It is highly improbable that the end of the barrel *he* made had a leak in it. The leak must have been in the top of the cask the end that the murderer made.

"There was no blood in the Bureau, or in the car, you remember. Yet such a blow on the head might well have caused some bleeding from the nose or from the wound. If the body had remained in the Bureau for any length of time, some bloodstains might have been found there. For the mallet was already in the Bureau, and, therefore, I suppose the crime was committed there.

"But the murderer dared not leave the body in a room with a window on a level with the ground. The door on the gallery was locked with a spring lock and could be opened without a key from, the Bureau side. The murderer's first instinct would be to drag the body through that door and conceal it in the *chai*. Once he moved the body out upon the gallery, he was no safer, for any one coming into the Bureau could open the spring lock as he had done and find the body on the gallery. If he dropped the body into one of the hogsheads, then full of must, it would be discovered within a few days, even supposing that it sank to the bottom of the vat.

"The only other concealment offered in the *chai* was, of course, one of the unfinished casks immediately below the gallery. Nothing could be simpler than to drop the body from the gallery into one of the casks standing open below. It was evidently dropped headfirst, as is shown by the position of the body in relation to the leak in the cask. Also, you remember, the Vicomte's watch was found not in his pocket, but lying in the cask near his head. When he was dropped from the gallery, the watch slipped from his waist-coat pocket and fell into the cask with such force as to stop the movement of the works. The broken watch crystal and the dent in the case make it certain that the drop was what stopped the watch, not the wine introduced into the cask some hours later.

"Probably the murderer ran down the steps and placed the head of the cask over the body. But for some reason, either through terror of interruption or anxiety to establish an alibi for that moment, he decided to return later and seal the cask, as we know he actually did. The thumping which Marty heard was evidently the noise made by the murderer when hammering the hoops onto the cask."

"I wonder why he did not wait until later, when every one would be asleep?" I said.

Congreve explained, "I think we may agree that there are several possibilities: first, the terrible nervous strain and suspense until the cask was finished; second, the fear that the noise he made in the *chai* would be more noticeable in the silence after midnight; and third, perhaps the fear of interruption by some member of the dinner party or of the household staff."

"The murderer would want to get that job done in a hurry, I see that," I agreed. "But isn't there a chance that the one who put the body in the cask did it to shield some one else?"

"That is a possibility, certainly," Congreve answered, sipping his wine.

"Well," I said, "it all hangs together, as you tell it."

"No other theory will explain all these circumstances," said Congreve.

"Well," I said, "if the man who murdered the Vicomte was the same fellow who concealed his body in the cask, Arno is your man. Lewin is bald headed. Fugger Bey and Monkhouse are both blonds. The man who killed Madame had black hair, you remember."

"Don't jump to conclusions, Merton," Congreve cautioned. "Marty said the murderer's *head* was black. It was not necessarily black hair that he saw."

"But surely," I objected, "Marty would not have confused hair with a black hat?"

"Certainly not," Congreve admitted. "But you must not forget the Gascon's black cap. You remember that it has not been found in the *chai*. Yet he left it there when he went off to dinner yesterday."

"What do you make of the blue blouse? That was left in the *chai*."

"So it was," said Congreve. "I take it the murderer put on the blouse as a protection against wine-stains or perhaps bloodstains—

during his work on the cask. It was absolutely essential that the cask be not only finished, but filled with wine and placed in position at the end of the row before morning. The murderer could not afford to risk winestains or bloodstains on his dinner coat, of course. He would naturally put on the blouse, and perhaps the cap also, if he feared interruption and wished a complete disguise. We must remember that only the *maître de chai* was supposed to have a key to the *chai*. If, then, any one saw a light and investigated, such a disguise would be very useful."

"But the Englishman said he had a key to the *chai*. He told us how Madame picked his pocket."

"Frankly, Merton, I do not believe that story. I knew Eugéne too well. Monkhouse had no such key."

"Well, then," I asked, "whom do you suspect?"

"Perhaps," said Congreve, "we had better eliminate those we do not suspect, first of all. Miss Simpson is obviously off our list. She knows nothing and is patently incapable of any crime requiring such skill and address. Mrs. Lewin is bitter enough and possibly unbalanced enough to commit a crime under sufficient provocation. But much as she hates Europeans and good wine, she has a horror of blood shed, due to her sorrow over the loss of her son. This should rule her out, in my opinion, even if she had no alibi. Marty's story stands up too well, in the light of what we know, to make it possible that he killed Madame Fürst, and certainly he was not in league with any of the other men except Lewin, and Lewin had no motive. He already had everything he wished and was on excellent terms with the Vicomte. The fact that the Vicomte shook hands with him as he did, using the hand nearest the heart, proves that."

"It proves only that the Vicomte was on excellent terms with Lewin."

"Superficially, you are right," Congreve assented, "But you are profoundly wrong. Eugéne was a great judge of men—if not of women. Besides, the crime was certainly committed *after* Lewin left the Bureau. If, as he says, two other men were there when he left the Vicomte safely in the car, he cannot have killed the Vicomte."

"His alibi saves him by a very narrow margin, then."

"That is true, but in my opinion he is in the clear. The *maître de chai* lacks an alibi for the murder of Madame. But he has one for the hour his master was killed. He was in the servants' hall from before that on until after dinner. His loyalty to his master sufficiently accounts for his first refusal to help in my investigation, as he evidently thought it possible the Vicomte was involved. The change in his manner since the discovery of his master's body satisfies me on that point. The other servants have all accounted for their time satisfactorily. It follows that, if the murder was committed by some person, or persons, known to be present in the Château, the guilty must be among the remaining three guests: Arno, alias Goosey Rauh, or Fugger Bey, or Monkhouse."

"All three of them might have been in it," I said.

"First, second, and third murderers again, Merton. I remember, you first proposed that theory."

"It was Marty's theory," I objected. "If you accept part of his story as true, you can hardly discard the rest."

"Don't be ridiculous, Merton," said Congreve, shaking his head. "If I accept certain of his statements for good and sufficient reasons, it need not follow that I must accept all statements he may make, without reason.

"Have a glass of this excellent wine and clarify your thinking.

"What was it Marty told us? Let us sift the facts and see if they necessarily establish his conclusion that there were two or three or possibly four persons in the *chai* when Madame Fürst was murdered."

"Well," I said, "he saw one man run up the stairs and hit her."

"Murderer Number 1," Congreve checked it off on his fingers.

"Second," I went on, ignoring his levity, "Marty heard somebody running on the stairs, and immediately after, the door on the gallery banged shut."

Congreve bent down a second finger.

"Murderer Number 2," he checked.

"Right after that, Marty heard somebody scuttling along the main floor between the barrels, and right away he heard the little door to the vineyard creak open and shut again."

Congreve nodded. "Your memory is excellent, Merton. Murderer Number 3."

"Finally, Marty heard the door to the bureau, the outer door, bang shut again. He thought Madame Fürst had done that."

Congreve, still smiling, turned down a fourth finger.

"Murderer Number 4," he said.

"We heard that door bang ourselves, you remember," I went on.

"Quite so," Congreve agreed. "But certainly Madame Fürst did not bang it. Now what's your theory of what really happened?"

"I suppose the actual murderer, who struck Madame Fürst down on the stairs, afterward ran into the Bureau, and was followed, soon after, by his accomplice, whom Marty heard on the stairs. The second man banged the gallery door after him."

"Which of the two banged the outer door on leaving the Bureau?"

"Of course, one can hardly say. Probably they waited there a few minutes to make sure the coast was clear."

"And then," Congreve prompted, "what next?"

"The third man, knowing that the door on the gallery would lock itself, and having no key, then scuttled down the aisle between the barrels to the little door into the vineyard. The key to that door, you remember, was on the inside. I saw it yesterday afternoon after Monkhouse let himself out. Fearing pursuit, the third man locked the door on the outside and made himself scarce."

"I wonder," said Congreve, "why you are so sure the third man had no key to the door on the gallery?"

"Well," I said, "the only key to that door was on the Vicomte's key ring then in the outer door of the Bureau, where we found it. Once that door on the gallery was banged shut, the man under the gallery was locked in. He had to get out through the vineyard."

"Fair enough, Merton. But now consider: suppose we assume that there was only one man involved in this crime?"

"How can you? Three doors are heard—three men are heard."

"No, Merton, I cannot agree. Consider the psychology. The man who struck down Madame Fürst heard Marty's noise in the loft and suspected that he had been observed. Very sensibly, he at once extinguished the light, instead of looking around to see where the noise came from. His first thought must have been to get out of the *chai*."

"Precisely," I agreed, "and the nearest door led from the gallery into the Bureau."

"Ah, yes," Congreve interrupted, "but his object was to get out of the *chai*, not *into* the Bureau. Madame Fürst had just come through the Bureau, leaving both doors open. For all he knew, her scream might have been heard by some one in the Bureau or just outside. In all probability, the murderer had no means of knowing whether she had come alone. In the circumstances, the door into the Bureau was the last exit he would choose."

"But Marty said," I protested, "that he heard the second man on the stairs just before the door banged shut. If the murderer did *not* pass through the door into the Bureau, there was no occasion to shut it, for it could be easily opened from the other side without a key. Of course, he might have done so in a panic. But if he did close it without entering the Bureau, what became of him afterward?"

"Just my point," said Congreve. "The man Marty heard on the stairs was the murderer. Marty assumed that the man was running *up* the stairs, whereas it is obvious that he was running *down*."

"But if he ran down the stairs, our murderers are reduced to three."

"To two, Merton; really to one."

"Explain," I demanded.

"It must have been like this. The murderer ran down the stairs and scuttled along the aisle to the only other exit open to him. Thus, what Marty took to be three separate men was really only one. Because he heard three voices, he assumed there were three persons beside Madame, whereas I am certain that he heard only two persons speaking and that one of these was Madame herself, who was necessarily dead before the murderer turned to fly.

"The truth is that the murderer ran up the stairs after Madame, struck her down, then rushed down the stairs, down the aisle between the barrels, and let himself out by the door into the vineyard. The door on the gallery, you remember, banged shut *after* the sound of running on the stairs."

"Well," I said, "that's very pretty, but who shut that door?"

"Nobody, Merton. That is to say, no human agency. You remember the wind was rising. Madame had left both doors open. Marty had left the loft open. It happened that the inner door was banged shut first, then, soon after, the outer door. If our three voices were two persons only, and if one of them was knocked in the head, it is manifest that there could have been only one man in the *chai*—the man who murdered Madame. If the murderer had gone out through the Bureau, would he have left the door open and the keys in it? No, he would have locked the door and taken the keys."

"Well," I agreed, "you make it seem possible, at any rate. But why on earth did the poor woman go into the *chai* in the first place at that time of night?"

"That can only be a matter for conjecture," Congreve answered. "Her habit of calling the lover of the moment 'Danilo' makes it impossible to say just whom she was looking for. Certainly she was anxious to establish a profitable connection with some one of the four men with whom she had been dallying. Monkhouse had cut down her allowance, presumably because of her fickleness. Arno had insulted her in public—for reasons best known to himself. Fugger Bey could not afford such an expensive woman or keep her for any length of time, while the Vicomte had shown a most unsympathetic spirit towards her earlier in the afternoon.

"Evidently, when she entered the *chai*, she did not know that the Vicomte was dead. Her alarm and her flight prove that beyond any reasonable doubt. She might, therefore, have come there looking for him—going first into the Bureau and afterward, hearing the noise in the *chai*, she may have looked for him there. If she had any means of knowing that Lewin had removed the Vicomte's financial difficulties, this is a very reasonable hypothesis.

"On the other hand, she may have had an assignation with any of the other three men, or it may be that the Danilo she found in the *chai* was not the Danilo she went looking for. I cannot see that we are ever likely to know her real motive in going there. None of these men can be expected to come forward with any information of that sort. It would be too incriminating."

"There is another thing I don't understand," I went on. "That cask in which the Vicomte's body was found—who moved it? I could have sworn it was in place at the end of the row when we found Madame and Marty last night. It must have been there if it leaked out enough wine to make her slip as she turned to run up the stairs. Yet it was not in place on our second visit. The Gascon claimed there were no fresh tracks in the mud. Then who moved it?"

"The Vicomte moved it."

"The Vicomte!" I exclaimed. "Don't be silly. The Vicomte was dead."

"No," said Congreve, "I mean it. The cask, as you know, leaked badly. It had been rolled into place at the end of the row where the new casks, just filled, were. You may have observed that no racks had as yet been made for these new casks. The Vicomte's body was wedged in and necessarily lay not along the axis of gravity of the cask. When the wine had drained out, the weight of his body being to one side caused the cask to roll over. That is why we found the leak on the top of the cask."

"Then, if it had been on its rack, the body would not have been discovered for three or four years, in all probability."

"No, no," said Congreve. "The wine is racked every three months here—drained off into new casks to clarify it and get rid of the lees. The body would certainly have been discovered in the cask before Christmas."

"Then the murderer had three months in which to dispose of the body?"

"Yes," said Congreve, "—if only he had been a better cooper."

CHAPTER II
A GRAND BOTTLE

IT WAS ALMOST MORNING when the door opened, and Monkhouse came in. He tossed his hat on a chair and sat down wearily.

"Well, gentlemen," he demanded, "any solution?" It was clear from his manner and tone that the question was wholly rhetorical.

"You flatter me," Congreve replied. "Far from it. Have you any news?"

"Yes and no," Monkhouse answered. "I buzzed into Bordeaux, as you suggested, and called at the notary's. But the fact is, the Vicomte hadn't been heard of there. I visited his club, his favorite café, and made some inquiries at the houses of his friends. Wasted a lot of time there, of course, because every one who is any one is at his Château for the vintage now. But the fact is, my search was hopeless. If my uncle went to Bordeaux, he must have gone into hiding."

"Did you ever consider the possibility that he may not have gone to Bordeaux at all?"

"You mean he's done a bunk?" the Englishman demanded.

"No. Not that," Congreve explained. "But his chauffeur returned and reported that when he reached Bordeaux, the car was empty. Apparently, the Vicomte never left the Château. His portfolio was in the car, and there were no indications that he had met with an accident. In fact, I am quite certain that Eugéne never went to Bordeaux."

"Ridiculous," the Englishman declared. "What makes you think so?" Deliberately, Monkhouse began to fumble for his pipe and pouch.

Congreve paused and studied the Englishman's bored face before he answered. "The fact is, Monkhouse," he explained, "your uncle was murdered!"

The Englishman's long face flushed and paled again, and the corner of his mouth twitched, as though with some nervous affliction ordinarily held under control. His hands, which had been busy in his pockets fishing for his pipe and pouch, rested idle for a moment.

"Murdered!" he repeated. "Good Lord! How do you know?"

"I found his body sealed in a cask in the *chai* while you were looking for him in Bordeaux." Briefly, Congreve narrated what had passed during the Englishman's absence.

"How appalling!" Monkhouse fumbled nervously, and this time his long fingers brought out pipe and pouch, and soon had the tobacco burning. Nonchalant as he had been about the killing of Madame Fürst, the murder of his uncle seemed to unnerve him. "How appalling!"

"Yes, isn't it?" Congreve agreed. "What do you make of it?"

"I?" Monkhouse replied, inhaling deeply. "Aoh, it baffles me, absolutely. I'm no sleuth, you know. I can't think when it could have happened."

Congreve announced, positively, that there could be no doubt about the hour of the murder. "Eugéne's watch was in the cask with his body, badly shattered. The hour at which it stopped was seven twenty-six. Obviously, he was murdered only a few minutes before that time, for we saw him in the courtyard only a few minutes earlier."

"Mm," the Englishman nodded. "Well, I must say you've done jolly well. I suppose we're all suspects now?"

"Not all," Congreve countered. "My list of suspects is considerably shorter than it was when you left for Bordeaux."

"I suppose you'll be calling in the police now," the Englishman offered.

"I was waiting to see what you advised," Congreve explained.

"I hardly know what to say," Monkhouse replied. "Of course, our plan was to carry on until my uncle turned up. But now you've turned out to be such a sleuth, I'm afraid I can't advise you, really. No doubt, the police ought to be called in. They must be before long, in any case. But I suppose if I am one of your suspects, I'd better express no opinion. Whatever we say may be used against us—you know the formula," he replied.

Congreve nodded. "All the same, I should like to ask you a question. When you found Madame Fürst going through your clothes, did you notice anything peculiar about her costume or appearance?"

"Rather," said the Englishman. "She looked as if somebody had been mauling her—tousled and bruised, you know. Jabbed in the eye, I suspected."

"Did she have her cloak with her?"

The Englishman considered, sucking his briar. "Perhaps she did; I can't be sure. No, by Jove, I don't seem to remember it. But I'm afraid my memory fails me absolutely on that point. It's not important, I hope? But, I say, it's already getting light. Aren't you frightfully fagged?"

"Not particularly," Congreve replied, yawning gently behind his hand.

"A man of iron, I see," Monkhouse replied. "Well, *I* am fagged. It is almost morning. I think I shall have a spot of coffee and go to bed for a bit. You won't be needing me soon, I suppose?"

"I think not," Congreve answered.

"Righto," said Monkhouse. "Cheerio!" and was gone.

When the windows were brightened by the morning light, I began to feel the effects of our long vigil, and the thought of alcohol as a stimulant became repugnant to me.

I ordered coffee with rolls and going into the dining room, sat down to breakfast. Congreve went in with me, but would taste nothing. I knew he could not abide French coffee. The silence in which we sat was soon broken by a shrill scream.

"What's that!" I cried. "Where did it come from?"

"It's a woman," Congreve answered, "upstairs. Come on."

Plump as he was, he kept well ahead of me as we hurried into the vestibule and up the broad stairs to the floor above. As we turned into the corridor on that floor, I saw Lewin, in his bathrobe, hurrying to meet us. Just before we met, he turned into an open door.

Congreve and I were right at his heels, but I confess that, once inside, I was a little embarrassed to discover that it was the bath, and that two ladies had preceded us. Mrs. Lewin was there, silent, frightened, but efficient, bending over the tub. In the tub, in her nightdress, sprawled Miss Simpson, limp and motionless. Her legs projected over the edge of the tub. She lay face downward. Beside her head, in the tub, lay a wooden mallet. I recognized it at once as the mallet used in the murders of the Vicomte and Madame Fürst. Mrs. Lewin was the first to speak.

"Richard," she said, "send for the doctor. The poor thing may be dying."

Reluctantly, Lewin backed out of the room, and I heard his slippers flapping as he bustled down the stairs, looking for a servant. Meanwhile, Mrs. Lewin and Congreve were busy with Miss Simpson.

"Whatever was she doing with that mallet?" Mrs. Lewin asked, of nobody in particular. "Poor thing, she's got a nasty bump on her head. She must have fainted in the tub. I hope it isn't serious."

"I don't think it is," said Congreve. "See, she's coming to, already."

Miss Simpson's head stirred slightly, and as we raised her and turned her over, her eyelids fluttered. We carried her into her room and laid her on the bed.

"It's only a bump on the head," said Mrs. Lewin, "though it has raised a big lump over her ear. She'll be all right in a little while, I think. Richard has sent for the doctor."

By the time the doctor arrived, Miss Simpson was all right, except for a bad headache. She could not account for her accident.

"I must have lost my balance and fallen into the tub," she said sheepishly. "I don't remember much about it."

Lewin followed us to the door of her bedroom.

"Did you see that mallet?" he said grimly. "That was no accident. She didn't fall into the tub. Somebody tapped her on the head.

Luckily Mamma went to the bath just at that time. Probably that scared the murderer away before he could finish the job. Where is everybody?" he demanded. "This has got to stop."

"Ah, yes," said Congreve, "and where were you when the poor lady was tapped on the head?"

"In bed, of course," said Lewin, "where any Christian would be at this hour."

"And where was Mrs. Lewin?"

"She was with me until she went to the bath, as I was just telling you," Lewin replied testily. His temper was none the better for his loss of sleep. "I'd just lain down when I heard the scream."

"You don't think Mrs. Lewin—," I put in.

Lewin interrupted me fiercely.

"Don't say it," he commanded. "She was in bed when I got there a few minutes ago. The mallet was in the *salon*, you remember, when I went upstairs. Mamma had nothing to do with this. Well, Mr. Congreve, what are you going to do?"

"I suppose," said Congreve wearily, "I shall have to ask every one in the Château for an alibi once more. The number of alibis in this Château is simply appalling."

Congreve's hunch was fully justified. We ferreted out every person in the Château and found, as he had expected, that every one had been in bed or asleep—though no one could prove it. We returned to the cold coffee in the dining room.

I attempted humor. "It was lucky for Miss Simpson that there was another American in the Château. You know the story about the cat that disappeared in the French hotel and was found three weeks later, starved to death, in the bathroom."

"That could hardly happen here," Congreve objected, with a faint smile, "even if there were no Americans. You mustn't forget that Monkhouse is an Englishman."

"But why should anybody try to kill Miss Simpson?" I demanded. "A more harmless ignoramus never lived. She can't know anything about these crimes. She couldn't kill a chicken. The mere news that a murder had been committed prostrated her yesterday, and she has been in her room ever since, on the far side of the house. The person who assaulted her must be a madman. Who do you suppose could have done it?"

But Congreve was not listening. His mind was apparently very far away, and a moment later he began to talk irrelevantly, as it seemed to me, upon his favorite topic.

"It is heresy to say so in Château Roet, Merton, but I know I may confide in you. Fine as the Bordeaux wines are, there is something a trifle too delicate, almost effeminate, about them. They are wines for the dilettante, for the trifler, for the man of pleasure—exquisitely adapted for their purposes. But where man is confronted with a practical problem, something more masculine is required. That is my experience, at any rate. If we were drinking merely for pleasure, if we were fresh and at leisure, I could ask nothing better than a Château Roet, or any one of the great growths of the *Médoc*.

"But this morning we are faced with a grave problem—a dangerous problem—which must be solved at once. If we had to fight, I should choose one of the great, full-bodied Burgundies or one of those massive and lusty vintages of the Rhone vineyards. But our enemy works in the dark, and we can foil him only with our brains. I prefer, therefore, a Burgundy of finer and more delicate character. Some wine whose deep color and rich abundance of bouquet striking our noses and palates with rapture will rouse our tired minds to their highest pitch of skill. We must have the right bottle.

"I propose Musigny. It is easily first in subtlety among the wines of the Côte d'Or. If Musigny 1906 will not solve our problem for us, we cannot hope to solve it. There is nothing in the cellar book which will so strengthen and clarify the brain."

Congreve moved over to the buffet and peered at the labels on the bottles. Suddenly he straightened and placed his hand upon one of them.

"Ah, here we are," he said, "there is the magic elixir, the philosopher's stone which will turn all our stupidities into wisdom. I trust *le bon Dieu* has not allowed this bottle to lose its potency."

Gently he brought the bottle to the table in its wicker cradle, and with dexterous fingers removed the capsule and drew out the cork. Swiftly he served the glasses, permitting no tilting back of the bottle which might disturb the sediment, and so foul the wine. With equal care, he went through the ritual of twirling his glass to release the marvelous bouquet. Then raising it to me, he gave utterance to a toast which was almost a prayer.

"Merton," he said, "to our success!"

"Merton," said Congreve with a sigh, after some minutes, "what do you make of it? Let's have your solution."

"There isn't any solution," I answered, with utter conviction. "I'm sunk, baffled, all at sea. The first two were bad enough, but this is insoluble. Anybody could have done it and nobody did. Yet it was done. I give up."

Congreve sat with his head between his hands.

"Is it possible I chose the wrong bottle after all," he muttered, as though talking to himself. "I was so sure—"

I was tired of his harping on the right bottle. "Right bottle be damned," I said. "There isn't any right bottle. I've drunk the same vintages you did all along, glass for glass, and I'm absolutely baffled. Your theory that good wine inspires good thinking is a lot of hooey, Congreve. It doesn't work out."

Congreve looked at me pityingly. Then his face suddenly lighted with a mischievous thought.

"Of course," he said, in a playful tone, "the wine can't do it all. There must be something there to inspire."

His levity and the implication of his remark nettled me. I was tired and sleepy.

"I'm not an utter fool," I countered, with momentary ill feeling.

Instantly Congreve was repentant. His face grew serious.

"Of course not. Can't I have my little joke?"

"As you put it, it's not a joke. I tried your method. It failed. There's only one conclusion."

"Ah," said Congreve. "Your logic is fallacious. You assume that the bottle that is right for me is necessarily right for you. A false inference. If you had chosen the wines for me, as I have for you, could I have solved the puzzles? I think not. You merely lack experience, Merton, my boy. Or maybe it's that rotten coffee."

I was not entirely mollified. Much as I liked Congreve, I could not refrain from the retort to which he had laid himself open.

"I can't see that you have entirely succeeded," I countered. "Who knocked Miss Simpson in the head? Tell me that, Mr. Know-It-All."

"I'm afraid I can't do that, Merton. This is baffling. Yet the bottle was right. I swear it was."

"Have another glass and think some more," I jeered at him.

But Congreve was again absorbed in his puzzle. My gibes never reached him, if he heard them.

"Yes," he said. "I'm baffled. Yet the problem is a simple one, surely."

"Too simple," I agreed.

Still he paid no attention to ridicule, but went on talking, half to himself.

"Merton, I insist that the bottle was right. If that problem could be solved, the inspiration of Musigny 1906 would solve it. I swear it would."

"But it doesn't," I persisted.

Congreve's face broke into a smile of triumph.

"Quite so. *Precisely!* How *stupid* of me! The thing is absolutely baffling." He positively crowed with delight.

"Merton, my boy, we're working against a very clever fellow. There's *no* solution."

I leaned back in my chair, disgusted, and stared at him in amazement. Had he gone loony with too much thought? Or was it too much wine?

"Yes," I said. "I see that he was a very clever fellow—far too clever for you."

He held up a hand in protest.

"No, no—not *too* clever."

"But," I insisted, "you admit defeat. You admit the problem is baffling."

Congreve was jubilant. "Of course, of course. It is perfect, it is baffling. It's meant to be baffling. The whole thing's a hoax, a red herring. I should have seen it *long* ago. Now I can get back to essentials."

I stared at him. "A very pretty explanation of your failure, Congreve. I thought better of you."

But Congreve was not to be cast down. "You're tired, Merton. Sleepy. I'm afraid you've had more wine than is good for you."

I was tired, I was sleepy. And his superior tone annoyed me, more especially as I knew I had a better head than his. I scowled at him, but in my wrath could think of nothing better than to reverse his comment. "You are the one who has had too much wine, Congreve."

False as that was, I hoped he would feel it. He has always prided himself on his moderation. I hoped to see his face redden; I expected him to lose his temper. But he did not.

Instead, he smiled sweetly and shook his head at me. "Don't be stupid, man," he urged. "Think back. How many glasses have I had since you came to the Château? In how many hours? You make yourself ridiculous. Seven or eight glasses at the most in twelve hours! With dinner, or before it—most of them. Not a liter, not one full bottle! My dear fellow, you'll have to think up something better than that!"

I had nothing to offer. I knew he was right. "I'm sorry," I mumbled.

"Skip it," he said. "Let's keep to the problem before us. It is really quite clear now. Don't you see? The assault on Miss Simpson was perfectly planned to deceive me."

"I see that," I agreed cynically.

"Yes," he nodded. "But good old Musigny 1906 and I have foiled the villain."

Congreve patted the moldy bottle with hearty affection.

"I may be stupid," I countered. "I confess I don't see."

"Oh, come now, Merton, you *must* see. The assault on Miss Simpson is almost a perfect reproduction of the murder of Madame Fürst. Both women are caught alone. Both are hit on the head with a mallet. In both cases, the mallet is left in evidence. Madame Fürst fell headfirst into the wine vat; Miss Simpson into the bath. It's a perfect reproduction."

"Not entirely," I objected. "The bathtub was practically empty. Miss Simpson was merely knocked out, not killed, and there was no chance of her drowning in the empty tub."

"Attaboy, Merton! The bottle was right, even for you. Your reasoning proves it. Don't you see? The murderer became more and more alarmed as our investigation went on. He saw me eliminating one suspect after another, until it had narrowed down to three or four. What can he do? By this time he knows that my methods are far more effective than the police are likely to be. He would be glad to have them called in before I can reach a solution. Accordingly, he plans to draw a red herring across the trail, put me off the scent, and keep me there, utterly baffled, under the illusion that I am hot on the trail of the murderer.

"In order to do this, he decides to commit a crime of a similar nature, so that I will believe that both were done by the same hand. That is why Miss Simpson got the mallet in the head and was heaved into the bathtub. But at the same time our criminal is getting cold feet. Clearly he has no intention of committing another murder. Therefore he offers a sham crime, unpleasant enough to Miss Simpson, in all conscience, but after all, in the long run, a small matter. He takes care not to kill her, not to let her drown. And he stages his little show at such a time and in such a way that every one in the party may be again suspected. He fooled you, Merton, he fooled me. But now we've caught him out."

"A very pretty theory, at any rate," I agreed grudgingly.

"Theory nothing, Merton. You have not found the right bottle."

CHAPTER III
CONGREVE COURTS DEATH

"MERTON," SAID CONGREVE, in a cheery tone which I found extremely irritating after being up all night, "our murderer is frightened. His assault on Miss Simpson proves that. What's more, he is *one* man, not two or three—the one man who knew all the details of the former crime. Still more important, we are now certain that he belongs in the Château. An outsider might conceivably have murdered the Vicomte and even Madame Fürst, but no outsider can have assaulted Miss Simpson. It was too carefully planned. She was tapped on the head by some one with a room upstairs on that corridor. It is one of the three Danilos. The question is—which one?"

"Yes," I said dully.

"We must get down to essentials. We must concentrate on the murder of the Vicomte. Madame Fürst was silenced of necessity; her murder cannot have been premeditated. The assault on Miss Simpson was merely a blind. We must concentrate on the murder of the original victim.

"Now the secret of a man's conduct lies either in his fears or his desires, or both. Arno wanted the vineyard. He feared exposure. Fugger Bey wanted Madame Fürst for his mistress, and to hold her he had to have money. Arno had hired him, but evidently the stipend was not sufficient to keep a woman so expensive as Madame. When it came to a choice between sacrificing that stipend or losing the favor of Madame Fürst, the Bey did not hesitate. He turned his back on Arno and went off with the woman.

Monkhouse also wanted his mistress and felt sure that she would return to him, as she always had done. But his money was his main consideration; I think we may take that for granted.

"Now as to immediate motive: the determination of the Vicomte to sell to Lewin instead of Arno would automatically throw the Bey out of his job, and this would entail the loss of his mistress. If he knew of that, he might have been driven to kill the Vicomte in the hopes that his son, the heir, would be forced to sell to Arno, or he might simply kill in the rage of despair.

"Now consider how the Vicomte's decision affects Arno.

"Arno had no real fear of Marty, I think. But if the Vicomte refused to do business with Arno, it meant exposure and probably deportation from France. Lewin and Marty were transients, but the Vicomte was a native, and could set the machinery of government moving to drive Arno from the country. No European nation would knowingly permit such a notorious criminal as Goosey Rauh to remain on its soil.

"As regards Monkhouse, his uncle's decision to sell to Lewin appears to offer less cause for malice. The money obtained from Lewin would settle the Vicomte's debt to Monkhouse. If he resented his uncle's change of plan, it must have been for some other reason—perhaps the loss of his commission on the sale, to be paid by Arno, or perhaps a fear that Arno would retaliate dangerously if the deal fell through. Thus, all three of these men had the opportunity to kill the Vicomte, so far as we can tell."

"Why not question them?" I threw in.

"No use in that," Congreve objected. "I wouldn't trust any of them as far as I could throw a feather. Each one would lie to shield himself and throw the blame on the others. Their evidence would be worthless. . . .

"As to capacity, the Englishman is a big, strong, sturdy fellow—something of an outdoor man. Arno, though smaller, is a gangster with many murders to his credit—a fiery-tempered, bloody-minded man, and armed. Fugger Bey is a former soldier, probably familiar with Turkish atrocities, used to evading the law, and quite capable of striking a man from behind. The mallet lay ready in the Bureau.

Whoever killed Eugéne must first have lured him back into the Bureau.

"Of course, I may be wrong in supposing that it was money or spite which motivated the murderer. This may have been a crime of passion, as Jules believes. Every one of these men has been the lover of Madame Fürst. And once Lewin's money had restored the fortunes of the Vicomte, who had been her first lover, any one of them may have killed him out of jealousy.

"What happened, I believe, was this: The murderer persuaded the Vicomte to go back into the Bureau with him. Having tapped him on the head, it would only be necessary for the murderer to slip out, gently close the door of the car, reach through the car window, and tap on the partition behind the driver. The engine was running, the lights were on, and Henri was awaiting the signal. From his position at the wheel, the car door and the door of the Bureau were both invisible. I have made sure as to how the car was started, and any one of these men might have known the Vicomte's customary signal. Certainly, he was not killed in the car. There were no bloodstains there.

"Of course, there are obstacles to fixing the guilt on any one of these men. The Bey, cruel as he was, and infatuated with Madame, evidently felt fairly secure of her affections. It was merely a matter of finding the money to finance her. And anyway, how do we know that the Bey was informed of the Vicomte's deal with Lewin? As for Arno, his own deal with the Vicomte was virtually completed. It is hard to believe that Eugéne would voluntarily court danger by informing Arno of his change of plans, though he may have done so. Monkhouse, confident that Madame would return to him, now that he had ready money in his hand, and expecting that his uncle would keep the matter a secret from Arno, would appear to have no motive whatever for murder. As for the concealment of the body in the cask, any one of them might have done it in the expectation that it would remain undisturbed for months."

"How do you expect to clear up these points?" I demanded. "Do you hope to force a confession?"

"Not at all," said Congreve. "How can I? I have no authority. That will be a matter for the police when I have put my finger on the guilty man."

"But good heavens, Congreve," I objected; "how can you do that if you don't know all these facts?"

"You talk like old Daddy Lewin," Congreve announced good-humoredly. "You must learn moderation in your thinking, Merton. Facts are interesting only as they point to character, for character is destiny. It was the criminal's character which caused him to commit these murders, and it is through his character that I will find him. The facts are only interesting as they throw light upon that central problem."

"Be more specific," I grumbled. "For example—"

"For example, the criminal is obviously a man who cares nothing for the ancient tradition of Château Roet—a man to whom good wine is only a commodity—a man to whom the wine-lover is only a sucker."

"That might fit any of them," I said. "If Arno is willing to adulterate a fine wine; if the Bey thinks chemistry is the whole secret; if Monkhouse would be a party to a sale to such a rascal— That doesn't carry us far enough."

"Very true," Congreve agreed. "But the criminal must likewise be a man who cares nothing for wine personally—really cares *nothing* for it. Take the Bey, for example. We have discovered that he is by no means a rich man. A bottle of vintage wine with his dinner must be barely within his means. Yet he prefers to pursue a woman like Madame Fürst. He would rather have a woman like that—other men's leavings—than enjoy the finest bottle. That seems very significant to me. Just think of that. To be infatuated with an old trull with a painted face and the soul of a miser, when once a day he might taste youth again in half a bottle of Château Roet. The Bey is adolescent, I tell you. He lacks maturity—and he suffers from catarrh."

I laughed aloud. "Is his catarrh a part of his character?"

"But of course," Congreve proceeded, unabashed. "His catarrh appears to me the only palliation for his moral weakness. The poor devil has no nose.

"As for Arno, to him all alcohol is simply 'likker.' He hardly knows one end of a wine bottle from the other."

"And Monkhouse?"

"Monkhouse is an Englishman who orders Asperges de Metz for a wine dinner—and with vinegar! These are facts of real importance. Those minor details you are so curious about may be safely left to the police."

"Look here, Congreve," I said, "don't play the eccentric detective."

"Eccentric? You call *me* eccentric? My dear fellow, I assure you I am not eccentric. I am an honest, normal person. It is the murderer who is eccentric. And by his eccentricity we shall know him."

"I can't see that you're any further along, after all," I replied grudgingly.

"On the contrary," George contradicted me with perfect assurance, "my work is practically finished. One more bottle, and I shall announce my solution."

"Always another bottle," I groaned.

"Only *one* more bottle," Congreve corrected me. "I shall name the criminal at luncheon to-day."

"Have you been holding something back from me?" I demanded, in exasperation.

"Nothing," said Congreve calmly. "You know everything that I know about this business, probably more. There can be only one solution. I shall declare it at *déjeuner* to-day, over the port."

"Port!" I cried, in astonishment. "Port at luncheon?"

"Just that," said Congreve. "A fine old Cockburn 1900. I grant you one doesn't ordinarily care for port at midday. It's all a question of the right bottle, as I have told you repeatedly."

"I never heard that port was a stimulant to the intellect," I persisted. "I should have thought something less heavy, less powerful, something with more finesse would be more suitable in solving this tangle."

Congreve crowed with delight. "Aha, so you *do* accept my theory!"

"Well," I hedged, "I suppose I do, in part. But port—and at luncheon, too! You rascal, you know the solution already. Cut out the hocus-pocus and let me have it now."

Congreve shook his head decisively.

"Sorry, Merton," he said, "but things must be done decently and in order. The fact is, there are one or two details that have yet to be checked. But if all goes well, you may rest assured that I will deliver the criminal to justice at luncheon. The police shall have him after that. Unless . . ." He broke off.

"Unless what?" I demanded.

"Unless another murder is committed in the meantime."

"Another murder?" I gasped. "But you just said that the murderer had cold feet, that he had no intention of committing another crime."

"Precisely. He *had* no intention, as I said. His feet are undoubtedly cold, and they will be colder as soon as I have informed the company of my intention."

"You're not going to tell everybody of your plan!" I cried. "It will put him on his guard. If he's frightened now, he will be desperate then."

"Precisely," said Congreve. "I want him to be desperate."

"Good Lord, man!" I cried. "Don't be a fool. You're inviting an attempt on your life."

"I suppose I am," said Congreve, without enthusiasm. "It's all I can do in the circumstances."

"Don't be quixotic," I pleaded. "You can't do the Vicomte any good now, and Madame Fürst was nothing to you."

"I know that," Congreve agreed gruffly. "But still, there are wrongs to be righted. The Vicomte is gone, as you say, and I am not revengeful. But there's more at stake than that. My friend loved his vineyard. He held it as a sacred trust. I just can't let him down now. The police might never solve this problem. I must carry on."

"But you don't need to let everybody know about it. Work under cover, keep your intention dark until luncheon. Then, if you must risk it, I can be prepared. I will get a gun."

Congreve smiled at me in friendly fashion, but shook his head.

"You're a good sport, Merton," he declared, "But I don't intend you to take any risks. I shall make it clear that I alone know the answer. You'll be quite safe."

"I don't mean that," I objected hotly.

"I know you don't," said Congreve. "But I want you to keep out of danger. I will not be responsible for your safety too."

"Well," I declared doggedly, "I think it's a damn-fool notion, but if you insist, remember I'm with you every minute until this silly business is over. If they get you, they'll have to get me too, or pay for it."

"Bravo!" said Congreve, laughing. "You're making my little experiment seem quite heroic. But I don't mind saying that if you choose to stand by, I shall be glad to have your company. A controlled experiment is always more informative. However, there's one point I must caution you about. Everything depends on the right bottle. I must warn you not to touch my port, unless I say the word. Not a drop, understand?"

I was mystified, but my confidence in Congreve prevailed.

"Very well," I said, "not a drop. But I do wish you'd let me in on your secret. Then I could be on my guard."

"Sorry, Merton; I can't do it. It would only endanger your life. Your face is so expressive. If you knew the answer, you could not conceal the fact. Please don't insist," he urged, and would say no more.

"Hello," I said, "there's Lewin."

Congreve beckoned, and Lewin, sleepy-eyed and worried, came to join us.

"Lewin," said Congreve, "it is almost the hour of the *apéritif*. Merton and I are going to the café in the village for a *Cinzano*. I want you and Marty to stay with the ladies. See that Marty's Colt is really loaded, will you? And ask Mrs. Lewin and Miss Simpson on no account to leave their rooms until you call for them. They must stay together—and upstairs. You stay with them the whole time."

"Why, what's up now?" Lewin demanded.

"If you'll call everybody together here, I'll tell you. But first, give Marty and Mrs. Lewin their instructions privately. Then I have something to say to you all. Let's get every one together here for a moment."

Lewin agreed, and went off to carry out Congreve's orders. And within fifteen minutes, the company had been assembled in the *salon*.

"Ladies and gentlemen," said Congreve, "I have asked you to gather here for a moment, because I have an important communication to make. These crimes cannot be kept from the police much longer. Fortunately, that will not be necessary. I have solved the riddle.

"No one of you knows all the facts, and I have, therefore, not confided my solution to any one. All of you have been under suspicion, necessarily, and a very unpleasant time it has been for us all. But the suspense is now about to end. As you may know, it is my belief that the right quantity of the right wine produces effects upon the brain which enable it to work out any problem which can be solved by human wit. I have chosen the bottle which I believe will enable me to declare my final solution of this mystery without a possibility of error. I have broached the bottle, and the wine is now in this decanter on the buffet, as you see. That wine is for me alone, and I must earnestly beg you all, in the interests of justice, *not* to take any of it until I have named the guilty man at luncheon. It is now eleven o'clock, the hour of the *apéritif*. I and my friend, Merton, here, are going into the village. I trust that you will all be on hand when luncheon is served."

It was almost a mile to the village café from the gates of the Château, but the autumn morning was delightful. Congreve stepped along more briskly than was usual with him, and we were soon seated at a little iron table under an old yellow-awning which flaunted its cheery message: TOUT VA BIEN.

When the proprietor appeared and had greeted us, Congreve amazed me. He ordered nothing.

"Aren't you having an *apéritif?*" I asked, in surprise.

"No, I think not—for once in my life," he explained.

"You're not ill?" I queried anxiously. "You'd better see the doctor."

He smiled at my question.

"No, not yet," he answered cryptically. "But your suggestion is very timely, Merton. Suppose you remain here for a few minutes. The proprietor is an old friend of mine—a man of excellent judgment. Since you came here with *me*, you may count upon his cooperation. Go ahead and order. I think I shall run across the street and visit *M. le Docteur*."

I stared, but before I could demand an explanation, he was striding over the cobbles towards the brass plate upon the door of the local doctor. For fully half an hour, I remained sipping my *apéritif* and munching olives, with one eye on the building into which Congreve had vanished. At the end of that time, the door opened, he appeared once more, and came to join me.

"And what is the report of the medico?" I demanded.

"Oh, that," he said. "We agree that I am in the best of health."

"Come, now," I said, "don't be mysterious. Why didn't you take your *apéritif* as usual?"

Congreve raised his eyebrows. "Didn't you understand all along? I thought I told you I was having a decanter of Cockburn 1900 with lunch," he explained. "A rare old port, that, Merton. I want to be perfectly fresh when that is served. True pleasure in wines demands an heroic measure of asceticism. Moderation is the secret of happiness for the wine-lover, as for other men."

CHAPTER IV
IN VINO VERITAS

PROMPTLY AT THE appointed hour, the company assembled in the dining room of the Château for lunch. But Congreve and I were there before them. I was accustomed, of course, to the seriousness with which he regarded food and drink, for though he never hurried, he was never late. But this time, I was annoyed by his fussiness and the solicitude with which he hovered over his decanter of old port. One might have thought him a child with a stick of candy, or that his decanter contained the only Cockburn 1900 in the world. His solicitude seemed silly, for I was sure that no one in the party had the least desire to drink port with a luncheon obviously planned as a frame for French wines.

When the company had been seated, Congreve took his place. I sat on his left. Lewin was on his right. Opposite were Monkhouse, Fugger Bey, Arno, and Marty, in the order named. Placing the decanter and his empty glass before him, Congreve addressed the waiting company.

"Gentlemen," he began, "this lunch was planned at the request of my late friend, the Vicomte. As it happened, this was the last thing he asked of me, and I take it very kindly that you have all assembled as I suggested. In a sense, this feast is given in memory of my friend. The chef has done his best. And I feel sure that you will do his efforts justice.

"However, you know that I promised to divulge my solution of the mysterious murders committed here within the last twenty-four hours. Well, as all of you have necessarily been suspects, I am sure you will all prefer that I set your minds at rest before we begin.

"My investigation was attended by many handicaps, but through your kind cooperation and the inspiration of the excellent cellar of Château Roet, I have been enabled to arrive at a very definite and final solution. I propose now to give you a resumé of my investigation. The explanation is likely to be long and intricate, as many false clues arose which will have to be explained away. I believe I told you my experience leads me to believe that good wine clarifies my mental processes as nothing else can do. I trust that you will not be too impatient to allow me to sample the excellent port in this decanter before I begin my somewhat tedious and involved explanation. Perhaps some of you would like to share with me?"

Congreve looked around the table hopefully, with a hospitable smile. But no one in the company cared to accept his offer. Each in turn indicated his entire indifference, or repugnance, to the port.

"Well, then, gentlemen, I must ask you to pardon me," said Congreve, and removing the glass stopper from the decanter, he poured a little of the port into his glass. Replacing the stopper, he carefully raised the glass towards his nose and with half-closed eyes very gently inhaled the aroma.

"Ah," he said, "Cockburn 1900. A rare treat, and this old bottle has a bouquet all its own."

Holding the glass before his face, he rotated the stem between thumb and forefinger and remarked, "I must ask you to be patient, gentlemen. You know that wines with so much body require a little time to release their ethers and surrender their full aroma."

His deliberation was maddening to me, though I was motivated only by an impatient curiosity. How maddening it must have been to the guilty man and even to others who might fear a false accusation may be imagined. But Congreve seemed unaware of the tension of the company and continued twirling his glass as though he had no interest in the world but the bouquet of that wine.

Lewin was breathing heavily. Marty sat with his hand in his pocket. A vertical line cleft the forehead of the dark-browed, scowling Arno. Fugger Bey's smile was imperceptible, and his cold blue eyes showed through narrowed lids. Monkhouse puffed imperturbably at his straight-stemmed briar.

Lewin was the first to speak. "For God's sake, Mr. Congreve, let's have it. All this beating about the bush is driving me crazy."

"I'm frightfully sorry," said Congreve, raising his glass. "I suppose I appear to be behaving very selfishly. But really I thought the wine would help me to arrange my thoughts so as to save time in the end. I'll just take a sip or two and then let you have the whole story. Is that agreeable to every one?"

He glanced around the table once more. No one had any objection to his program.

"Let's go," said Arno hoarsely.

"Very well," Congreve agreed, and raised his glass as though to drink. Then, suddenly, an idea seemed to strike him.

"On second thought," he said, "I see no reason to keep you waiting that long. After all, the evidence I had to present is a matter rather for the police than for this company. Bits of the story are known to all of you already, but I alone have the thing worked out. What you all want is the name of the guilty man, I take it? After all, I may as well spare you the details. I can give them to the police later. Shall I come out with it—once and for all?"

"Let's get it over," Arno demanded.

"Very well," said Congreve, setting down his glass again, "but I must warn you—one of you is going to get a nasty shock. Of course, I have no authority. I'm only an amateur detective. I naturally prefer to take no risks in such a case. I must ask you gentlemen to place your hands on the table. The guilty man may be armed, for all I know. There's been quite enough killing here already."

All of the company laid their hands on the table as Congreve had requested. All, that is, but Marty. He got to his feet and backed from the table, one hand in his coat pocket.

"Not me," he objected fiercely. "You can't hang anything on me."

Lewin would have protested, but Congreve glanced at him and shook his head.

"Very well, then, Marty. Just as you will. If you are innocent, you have nothing to fear. And I may as well confess that you are not the guilty man. What I have to say is not the result of guesswork, I assure you. I know who the murderer is."

"All right. Then shoot," said Marty, without budging.

"Will no one join me in a glass first?" Congreve asked. Once more he glanced round the table, smiling hopefully. "If no one will drink with me, of course, I sha'n't drink."

Monkhouse extended his glass towards the decanter. No one else moved. Congreve poured some of the port into the Englishman's glass, and raising his own, clinked his glass with that of Monkhouse, and raised it towards his lips. Monkhouse held his glass under his nose and made a great show of enjoying the bouquet of the wine. Congreve also moved with a deliberation which exasperated us all.

"For Heaven's sake, Congreve," Lewin broke in, "if you're going to drink, drink it down. Don't keep us waiting."

"Bottoms up, Monkhouse!"

Monkhouse, however, seemed in no hurry. He did not drink. Congreve set down his own glass. The Englishman immediately followed his example.

"Well, Monkhouse," Congreve sighed, "I'm afraid the company is against us. I shall not keep you waiting longer, gentlemen. The guilty man sits opposite."

Congreve pointed with a plump forefinger. "Goosey Rauh, alias Everett Arno," Congreve said.

For a split second, Arno sat motionless. Then he jumped to his feet. But before he could grasp his weapon, Marty was upon him, thrusting his own gun into the small of Arno's back.

"Hands up, Goosey," he commanded triumphantly. "Hands up, or I'll plug you."

It was evident that Arno knew Marty too well to disobey. His hands shot into the air.

"You've framed me, damn you!" he screamed. "I never done it! You're no cop. You can't hold me."

"The hell we can't," said Marty fiercely, in his ear. "Tell it to the judge. You can't beat the rap in this country. I warned you."

Congreve, still seated, lifted a protesting hand. "Frisk him, Marty," he commanded, without raising his voice. "Take his gun."

Marty quickly obeyed and transferred the weapon of the gangster to his own pocket.

"You're sure he has only one gun?" Congreve cautioned.

"Yes, sir," said Marty. "That's all."

"Very well. Then step aside and let him go."

"Let him go?" said Marty.

"But, I say," said Monkhouse, "you're not going to let him go, are you? That's a bit thick, really."

The smile had come back to Fugger Bey's cold face. His blue eyes twinkled. Lewin sat relaxed, like a sack of meal.

"I'm afraid we can't do anything else, gentlemen. Mr. Rauh is quite right. I have no authority. I can only present my evidence to the police."

Marty protested, and it took the combined efforts of Lewin and Congreve to persuade him to step aside.

Arno lowered his hands and grinned malevolently at the Englishman.

"I'll get you for this, Monkhouse," he threatened.

"Shut up, you rat," Marty commanded. "Get going."

Without a word, Arno turned and deliberately made his way out of the dining room.

"Well," said Lewin, "I'm glad that's over. Are you sure of your ground, Mr. Congreve?"

"Quite," said Congreve, "I told you I knew who the guilty man was. But don't concern yourselves. The man is not dangerous now. The police are waiting for him in his taxi. It appears that he was interested in the illicit narcotic trade. His passport is a forgery. He won't get away. I telegraphed the *Sureté* immediately after finding Eugéne's body."

"Ach," said Fugger Bey, smiling contentedly. "You overlook nothing, Mr. Congreve. You are most thorough. You should belong to the *Sureté*."

Congreve ordinarily was the most modest of men, but, at that moment, he actually preened himself. I was disgusted at his display of vanity.

"You think so?" he purred, gloating.

"Splendid," said Monkhouse. "It was really very neat."

Congreve showed genuine pleasure at the Englishman's comment. "You think so?" he said, and his voice was delighted. "I shall remember that, coming from an Englishman. Every one knows that the English police are the most efficient in the world."

"Really, I mean it," said Monkhouse. "Scotland Yard would be proud of you."

"Well," said Congreve, "that was soon over. There's still a little time before lunch, I believe. Surely, now you won't say 'no' when I offer you a glass of my port. A drink around will do us good."

"But aren't you going to tell us how you solved the crime?" said Monkhouse, puffing his pipe. "I'm bursting with curiosity."

"What's the use?" said Congreve. "It's a long story and should go to the police first of all. Come, have some of my port, gentlemen."

Nobody responded. Even at that moment, the thought of a heavy port before lunch was too repugnant. Congreve turned to the Englishman.

"Come now, Monkhouse," he urged. "Surely, you won't let me down. I've always understood that all Englishmen drank a fiendish lot of port. Won't you join me?"

He passed over the decanter. Monkhouse laid aside his pipe and drew the stopper from the tall decanter.

"Of course," he said, "I'm frightfully fond of port, but hardly before luncheon."

"Oh, come now, Monkhouse. Don't be so finicky. This wine is excellent—your favorite, I should think."

"It's too heavy to take before lunch," Monkhouse objected.

"You can't mean that," Congreve insisted. "Every one knows that Englishmen prefer heavy, powerful drinks, and of them all, there's nothing like port. It warms one while it strengthens. Won't you join me?"

But Monkhouse hesitated. He applied his nose to his glass, then to the decanter.

"I'm afraid your judgment is at fault here, Mr. Congreve," he declared judicially. "This port doesn't seem quite right."

"Really?" said Congreve earnestly. Raising his glass, he inhaled gently once more.

"I believe you're right," he said. "It does have a curious bouquet—a little like peach pits. It was not perceptible before. I suppose the bottle has 'gone off', after all. Port sometimes does. Not much of it keeps even up to forty years. Too bad!"

Reaching out, he took the decanter from Monkhouse, and raising his glass, carefully poured its contents back into the decanter. Replacing the stopper, he called the butler.

"Robert, something seems to have gone wrong with the port," he said. "You don't suppose any one can have meddled with it?"

"I think not, sir," the butler replied.

"Well," said Congreve, "something's wrong. I wish you would lock the decanter up until I can make sure. Remember, this is *my* bottle. I want nobody to touch it, understand—nobody."

"Certainly, sir," the butler replied. "I shall see to it."

Obediently, he carried the decanter from the table and out of the room.

"Well, gentlemen," said Congreve, "since you don't like my port, I suppose we may as well have a drink of something else. Perhaps something stronger than wine would satisfy the company. How about an American cocktail?"

"Ah," said Lewin, "that's better. I know something about cocktails. After what we have been through, I should think nothing could be better."

"Good," said Congreve, rising. "Since you have scorned the port I offered, I insist, for the sake of my reputation, that you allow me to prescribe for you. How about a Buffalo Wallow?"

"A what?" Lewin demanded.

"You can't mean you don't know what that is?"

"I'm afraid not," Lewin confessed.

"Me, neither," said Marty, "but let's go."

"It won't spoil the wines?" said Fugger Bey, with a smile.

"Aoh, damn the wines," said Monkhouse, "let's have it."

"Bon," Congreve assented, and proceeded slowly to the buffet, where he began his work.

In a short time, he returned with a tray containing five glasses. We all sat down to enjoy a new experience. Meanwhile, Robert re-appeared.

"It's potent, I warn you," Congreve said, as he served us each in turn. "But I imagine we can all do with a bracer."

Seating himself once more, he raised his glass. "Bottoms up," he urged. "It's the only way to drink a Buffalo Wallow."

The glasses clinked, and we all obeyed his instructions.

I must confess I was somewhat disappointed with the new drink. It seemed to me to be simply a rather weak Martini. But knowing Congreve's pride in his connoisseurship, I made no comment.

The Englishman coughed.

"That's a rouser," he declared positively. "You Americans have stomachs of brass."

"And now," said Congreve, "it must be time for lunch. For my part, I'm ready for it."

At his signal, the butler disappeared. But apparently the chef was not ready. There was a considerable wait, which we had to endure as best we could. Even the cocktail seemed not to be enough to raise our spirits after the suspense we had endured.

Congreve employed the time questioning Fugger Bey.

"I suppose you don't mind answering a few questions for me, now that the guilty man has been exposed?" he said.

Fugger Bey smiled. He sat at his ease, evidently warmed by the cocktail he had drunk.

"Not at all," he replied.

"Good," said Congreve. "There are certain points you were rather vague about before, and others on which I had no time in which to question you. Do you mind telling me exactly what you did after you entered the door of the Bureau just before the Vicomte's car drove away?"

"Certainly," the Bey agreed. "This is what happened: Arno and I came together to the Bureau, for Arno was anxious to go to Bordeaux with M. le Vicomte to see the notary. I fancy Marty's threat of exposure had alarmed him. He was very eager. Just as we entered the Bureau, Monkhouse came out and went up the stairs to his rooms. I don't know that Arno noticed, but I saw Monkhouse putting a great roll of bills into his pocket. Immediately, I suspected what had happened. That Mr. Lewin had stepped into Arno's shoes and relieved the Vicomte's anxieties. While Arno talked with the Vicomte, trying to persuade his host to take him along to Bordeaux, I was busy with my thoughts. Immediately, I realized that my association with Arno would be fruitless for me. I hardly knew what to do. It had happened so suddenly. I excused myself and went off into the garden to consider what to do.

"In the garden, I encountered Madame Fürst, who had agreed to wait for me there. I was tempted to inform her, but before I was quite sure of what I should do, Arno came hurrying out after me. Just as he reached us, I heard the engine of the car roaring under the archway, as the chauffeur started away. I had no desire to converse with Mr. Arno at that moment, but he came up and requested Madame to withdraw for a moment, and questioned me—seeming very suspicious.

"Of course, I had nothing to tell him; and after a while, he went back the way he had come, to find his taxi. I immediately rejoined Madame Fürst, and together we made our way through the gardens and along the path to the village. You know, it is much shorter that way. We had to make haste to dress for dinner.

"You know what happened at dinner that night. Arno was in a vile humor and insulted Madame. I had decided not to break with Arno for the time being. But when he affronted Madame Fürst, I could no longer be friends with him. I knew that his business here was ended.

"Madame and I immediately left. On the way through the courtyard, she reproached me for quarreling with Mr. Arno, saying that I had behaved in a foolish manner. I suppose, now, that she was hoping for a compliment from me—some further evidence of my devotion. Not understanding her attitude, I became enraged and told her what I knew.

"There I made a great mistake, for immediately she realized that Arno would be exposed and that I could not hope to receive the money which he had promised me for my services. The Vicomte

had been her first lover. His fortunes were now restored. She at
once abandoned me and declared she would go back to him. When
that happened, I was furious and beat her, as I told you. Naturally,
she ran from me as soon as she could escape. The Vicomte, she
supposed to be in Bordeaux. Naturally, she turned to her only other
protector in the Château, Mr. Monkhouse. I suppose she went into
his rooms."

Monkhouse broke in: "And picked my pockets, as I told you.
Fortunately, I found her there and made her disgorge—all but the
keys."

"Those are the Vicomte's keys we found in the door," Lewin
objected, with a puzzled look.

"No," said Monkhouse, "they were mine—a duplicate set. She
took them and let herself into the Bureau, I suppose. Hearing some
one working in the *chai*, she went on into it, looking for a friend."

"But," I said, "how did Arno get into the *chai?*" I thought I knew
all that Congreve knew about the business, but that baffled me.
"How about that, Congreve?"

"It's all perfectly clear to me now," said Congreve, "but these
details must be saved for the police. Aren't they ever going to serve
luncheon?" he complained irritably.

Apparently, the butler had forgotten us, and we waited with
such patience as we could command. Lewin was uncommunica-
tive. Marty sat silent, waiting to feel the effect of his liquor. I fought
with myself to keep from asking for a second glass, while Congreve
entertained Monkhouse, talking interminably and in great detail
of the formulæ of all the cocktails known to man.

Monkhouse joined in the conversation at first, but soon appeared to be bored with it and withdrew into himself, looking
around the table groggily. Suddenly, he got unsteadily to his feet,
declaring he felt sick. He leaned with both hands on the table, sway-
ing a little, and then, very slowly and heavily, slumped down into
his chair again. His glazing eyes rolled towards Congreve, who remained motionless, smiling at him.

"You—you," the Englishman mumbled.

Then his head fell forward on the white cloth.

"Hello," said Lewin, "Monkhouse has passed out."

"Yes," said Congreve placidly, "so I see. I'll call Robert."

Taking his knife from the cloth, he tapped his glass twice with the metal. Immediately, the door of the butler's pantry opened, and two gendarmes in uniform stepped into the room.

"Good day, Inspector," Congreve said, in French. "There's your man."

"Good day, Monsieur," the officer replied. "Is he drunk?"

"One of our American cocktails was too much for him, Inspector," Congreve replied. "You'd better take him now while he can offer no resistance. I accuse him of the murder of my friend, the Vicomte, and of the murder of Madame Fürst. He is also guilty of an assault upon Miss Simpson and an attempt upon my life. If you will look in his pockets, I think you will find Mr. Lewin's money and the key with which Monkhouse let himself into the Bureau during dinner to conceal the body of his uncle."

Swiftly, the gendarmes searched Monkhouse. Everything was as Congreve had foretold.

When the confusion their coming had made had abated, and the gendarmes had carried Monkhouse away, Lewin and I plied Congreve with questions.

"Great guns!" said Lewin. "How many more of us are guilty? You're not planning on sending us all to the guillotine, I hope?"

Congreve replied, "No, Lewin, Monkhouse is the real murderer. I only accused Arno to expose him and to punish him for having planned the ruination of the good wine of Château Roet. The fact is, I had eliminated all my suspects but three. Of the three, Arno seemed least likely to be the guilty man."

"Why?" Marty demanded.

"You should know that," Congreve answered. "In the *chai* in the afternoon, you recognized Arno by his voice. Yet in describing the three voices in the *chai*, you never once recognized the voice of Arno. When you think of it, *that* would seem to eliminate Arno."

Marty had nothing to say to that. It floored him.

Congreve turned to the German.

"You understand, of course," he said, "that I had to consider you as the possible murderer?"

"Certainly," said the Bey, smiling, "I understand."

"You see," said Congreve, "I knew that all three of my suspects— Arno, the Bey and Monkhouse—had a considerable knowledge of chemistry. The Bey had been engaged in smuggling drugs and in chemical warfare. Arno, or perhaps we should call him Rauh, had been a big shot in the illicit trade in narcotics in the States. Monkhouse owned a factory where chemicals were manufactured. I knew that the guilty man must be desperate, as he found his crimes uncovered, one after another, in rapid succession, and that an attempt on my life would logically be his next step. The opportunities for killing me in secrecy were strictly limited. I assumed, therefore, that he would try to poison me. Accordingly, I made the attempt easy for him by decanting the port and leaving the decanter on the buffet for some hours before lunch.

"In order to keep the coast clear for his operations, I asked the ladies to remain in their rooms, got Lewin and Marty, here, out of the way, and went off with Merton to have an *apéritif*. Robert saw to it that the servants kept away.

"While in the village, I visited the local doctor, obtained a few crystals of chloral hydrate to make our murderer harmless, and glanced through a book on toxicology in his little library. When I returned, a few whiffs of the wine convinced me that he had poisoned it with hydrocyanic acid. There was a perceptible odor of bitter almonds—very faint, but perceptible. Of course, that poison is very volatile, and soon leaves little trace when exposed to the air. Therefore, I chose port, because its body would delay the evaporation of whatever volatile poison might be introduced into the decanter.

"Of course, I never had any intention of tasting the wine in that decanter, and merely used it to test out the criminal's reactions. As a matter of fact, I was already satisfied that Monkhouse was the guilty man without that, and merely used it for corroboration of my conclusion."

"How did you know?" Lewin demanded.

"Why, you see," Congreve explained, "Monkhouse was the only one of the three suspects who was not present when I demonstrated my skill in identifying old wines by their bouquet and flavor before dinner last night. Surely, any one present at that time would have had more sense than to use a poison with such a pronounced odor. The moment I whiffed it and recognized the smell of bitter almonds, I knew that Monkhouse was my man. But I wanted to expose Arno and run him out. Also, I chose to verify my conviction by playing a game with Monkhouse over the wine.

"You remember that at first he was willing to wait while I drank, but when I had declared Arno the guilty man, he was unwilling to have me drink before I had presented my evidence to the police. That convinced me that he knew the wine was poisoned. In his pocket, as you saw, the gendarmes found his own key to the Bureau; the keys Madame Fürst used were the Vicomte's. It is perfectly clear that after the Bey and Arno had gone into the garden, Monkhouse came down the stairs with the notes, lured his uncle into the Bureau, and while he was putting them in the safe, murdered him there. He took his uncle's keys, concealed the body, and went to dress for dinner. Unfortunately for him, he left his uncle's keys in his tweeds. Madame Fürst came in later, in his absence, and found them in his clothes. When he discovered that she had used them, he had to pretend that they were his own keys—a duplicate set—taken from his clothes."

"But why?" I demanded.

"In order to account for his delay in returning to the dinner table," Congreve explained. "Surely that is obvious. That was why he made up the yarn about finding her in his rooms."

"But the motive? What could be his motive? His uncle had paid him in full, and he could have had his mistress again," Lewin insisted.

"No," said Congreve, "you're wrong there. Monkhouse was a spendthrift—deeply in debt. That was why he had to press his uncle for payment—why his mercenary mistress left him. With Lewin becoming a partner in the vineyard, Monkhouse knew that Madame

Fürst would turn to the Vicomte again. Of course, Monkhouse was
not the man to commit a murder merely for a mistress. The fact is,
he was in terror of his life. He feared Arno, for Arno had paid him,
in advance, a considerable commission on the sale of the vineyard,
which he had arranged."

"Well," I said, "he certainly was cool. I've heard that Englishmen were imperturbable, but this one surpasses all my expecta-
tions."

"Ah," said Congreve, "but he had a means of inducing states of
mind, as well as I."

"What?" I demanded.

"A magic wand," Congreve replied, smiling.

"Come now, don't be mysterious. What was his magic wand?"

"His pipe was his magic," Congreve explained. "A magic which
turned a turbulent, unstable spirit into one of utter coolness. You
must have observed how excitable he was without his pipe—how
calm when puffing it. Do you suppose," Congreve went on, with
real annoyance, "that I would have tolerated his damned tobacco
at a wine dinner, if it had not been necessary? Such men deserve
to be hanged."

COACHWHIP PUBLICATIONS

COACHWHIPBOOKS.COM

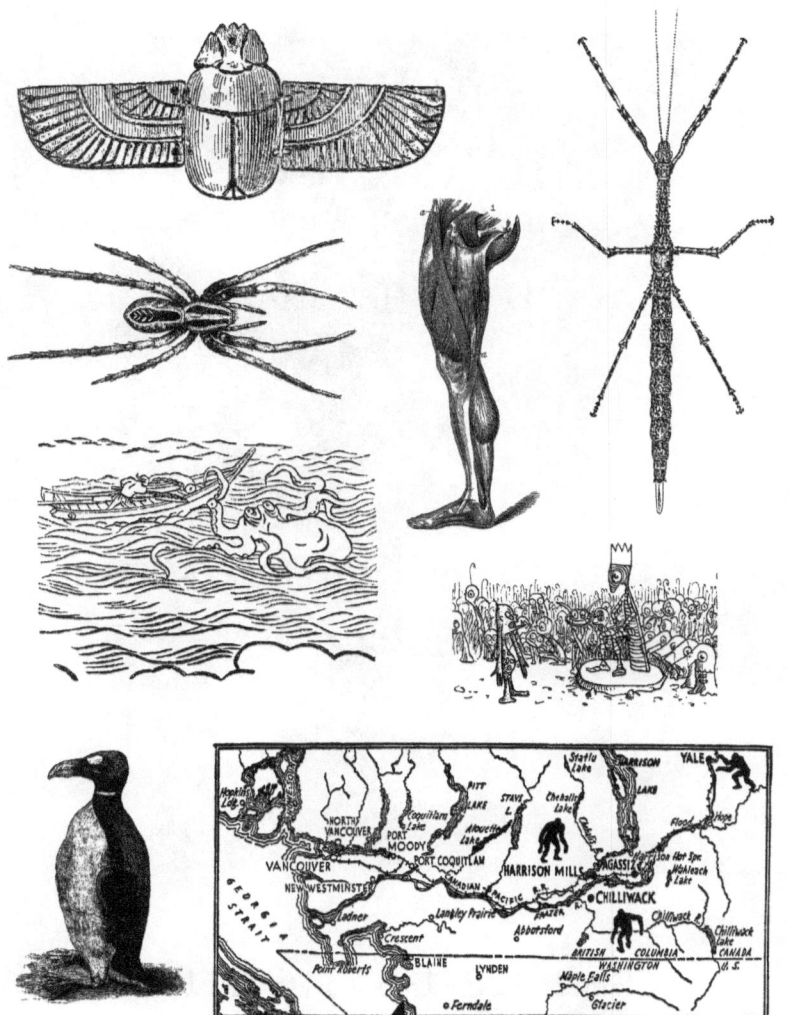

COACHWHIP PUBLICATIONS

COACHWHIPBOOKS.COM

MURDER OF
THE HONEST BROKER

WILLOUGHBY SHARP

ISBN 978-1-61646-211-6

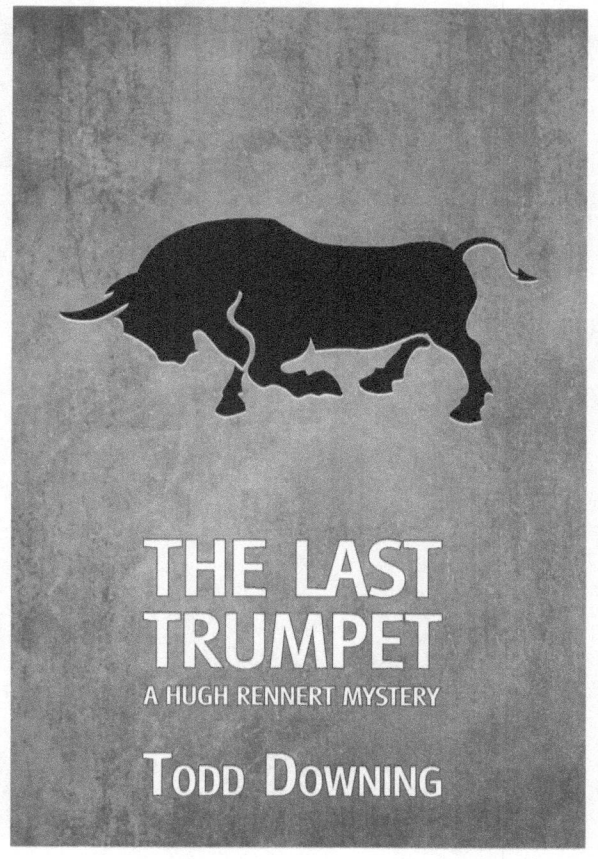

ISBN 978-1-61646-152-2

COACHWHIP PUBLICATIONS

COACHWHIPBOOKS.COM

CLUES AND CORPSES
The Detective Fiction and
Mystery Criticism of Todd Downing
CURTIS EVANS

ISBN 978-1-61646-145-4

THE STRAWSTACK
MURDER CASE
KIRKE
MECHEM

ISBN 978-1-61646-179-9

COACHWHIP PUBLICATIONS

COACHWHIPBOOKS.COM

MURDER

À LA RICHELIEU

THE ADELAIDE ADAMS MYSTERIES

ANITA BLACKMON

ISBN 978-1-61646-222-2

www.ingramcontent.com/pod-product-compliance
Lightning Source LLC
Chambersburg PA
CBHW020648260626
47157CB00008B/2958